C000233944

100 Reasons to Celebrate

We invite you to join us in celebrating
Mills & Boon's centenary. Gerald Mills and
Charles Boon founded Mills & Boon Limited
in 1908 and opened offices in London's Covent
Garden. Since then, Mills & Boon has become
a hallmark for romantic fiction, recognised
around the world.

We're proud of our 100 years of publishing
excellence, which wouldn't have been achieved
without the loyalty and enthusiasm of our
authors and readers.

Thank you!

Each month throughout the year there will
be something new and exciting to mark the
centenary, so watch for your favourite authors,
captivating new stories, special limited
edition collections…and more!

Available in March 2008
from Mills & Boon® Intrigue

Desert Justice

VALERIE PARV

MILLS & BOON
Pure reading pleasure

First published in Great Britain 2008
by Harlequin Mills & Boon Limited,
Eton House, 18-24 Paradise Road, Richmond, Surrey TW9 1SR

© Valerie Parv 2006

ISBN: 978 0 263 85944 7

46-0308

Harlequin Mills & Boon policy is to use papers that are
natural, renewable and recyclable products and made from
wood grown in sustainable forests. The logging and
manufacturing processes conform to the legal environmental
regulations of the country of origin.

Printed and bound in Spain
by Litografía Rosés S.A., Barcelona

To Drew, with thanks for his generosity, and to
my agent, Linda Tate, for her patience
and belief in this story.

VALERIE PARV

With twenty million copies of her books sold,
including three Waldenbooks bestsellers, it's no
wonder Valerie Parv is known as Australia's
queen of romance and is the recognised media
spokesperson for all things romantic. Valerie is
married to her own romantic hero, Paul, a former
crocodile hunter in Australia's tropical north.

These days he's a cartoonist and the two live
in the country's capital city of Canberra, where
both are volunteer zoo guides, sharing their love
of animals with visitors from all over the world.
Valerie continues to write her page-turning novels
because they affirm her belief in love and happy
endings. As she says, "Love gives you wings,
romance helps you fly." Keep up with Valerie's
latest releases at www.silromanceauthors.com.

Dear Reader,

When I was a little girl, my family moved to Australia from England. My adopted country had different customs, accents, a different social structure and a landscape alien to anything I'd known, vast and untamed, the earth red where I'd only known green. Much as I loved (and still do) this wonderful frontier country, adapting was a challenge. Now I wouldn't live anywhere else, and have explored Australia from coast to coast with my husband, a former crocodile hunter, making fascinating discoveries at every turn.

This may explain why my heroines often find themselves in unusual settings or situations where they also have to sink or swim. Invariably, they swim, with a gorgeous man right alongside. In this book, I wanted to create a desert warrior worthy of a headstrong, capable Aussie heroine. His kingdom also had to be something special to equal *her* homeland. I hope you find both as enticing as she does.

Best,

Valerie

Chapter 1

From his hiding place among the ruins of the ancient castle known as Al-Qasr, the business-suited man studied the foreign tourist through powerful binoculars. He was almost disappointed to find that she wasn't the one he'd come to kill.

As she spoke boldly to a male guard, the watcher's lip curled in distaste. When he ruled Nazaar, such wanton behavior would be punished. Female beauty like hers would be hidden from men's eyes, saving them from the sinful lust he felt stirring in his loins.

Should he kill this woman, too, as an example to all temptresses? He touched the vial of poison in his pocket. There was enough for her as well as his intended target. Why not start as he meant to go on?

Simone Hayes felt her heartbeat quicken as she saw the motorcade arrive at Al-Qasr. As she'd hoped, the fleet of

Rolls Royce cars pulled up close to where a silk cordon separated the tourists from the royal party. Unlike the expectant crowd around her, she wasn't waiting for a glimpse of His Royal Highness Sheikh Markaz bin Kemal al Nazaari, hereditary monarch of Nazaar.

Nevertheless, her gaze was attracted by a pennant bearing the royal coat of arms fluttering from the lead car. Then the sheikh himself emerged from the vehicle. Unlike most of his entourage, Markaz al Nazaari had no beard to reduce the impact of a strong, unyielding profile that would have looked at home on a Roman coin. His upright bearing and assured movements suggested an enviable ease with who and what he was. Simone didn't need to be any closer to feel the air of absolute authority he projected.

Applause followed him as he was welcomed by the director of the Al-Qasr, an ancient fortress complex in the desert, now a popular tourist attraction. In contrast to the intense light, everything about the sheikh looked dark, from the glimpse of night-dark hair and brows visible under his traditional headdress, to his burnished olive skin. She couldn't see his eyes as he approached the receiving line, but she would bet they were dark, too. He looked about as relaxed as a trap waiting to be sprung, she thought with uncharacteristic fancy.

Out of professional interest, she itched to get a better look at the *mishlah* he wore over his white dishdasha. The *mishlah,* a transparent black surcoat with exquisitely embroidered gold edges, was only worn by royals, sheikhs and potentates. On his head was the haik, a long stream of white cloth held in place by an *i'qal,* a black band threaded with gold.

Taller than the men around him with the exception of a giant who stayed glued to his boss's side, the sheikh looked exactly how Simone had imagined a prince of the desert should look.

She had to make an effort to switch her attention to the guards and attendants surrounding the sheikh. Could her father's half brother be among them, as her inquiries had led her to hope?

Unfortunately, every one of the sheikh's party wore impeccable—and identical—white dishdashas, the traditional neck-to-ankle male garment in Nazaar. Only their roving eyes and the tiny black earpieces linked to wires disappearing inside their clothing distinguished them from the other Nazaari men she'd seen when she explored the ancient site earlier.

The man she sought had a distinctive tattoo of a coiled snake around his right wrist, but the sleeves of their dishdashas fell over the men's hands. How was she supposed to get a look at their wrists?

She hadn't expected to be so distracted by the sheikh that he and several members of his party were inside the main building by the time she snapped out of her reverie. Now what was she going to do? She'd already been told that no visitors were allowed inside while the sheikh inspected some recently completed restoration work on the famous tourist attraction. She would have to try again to spot her half uncle when the royal party emerged from the main building.

The inspection would last exactly forty-five minutes, she'd been told by an attendant, then the sheikh would be entertained to lunch under an elaborate marquee erected between the rose-colored buildings.

Around her the crowd was dispersing, heading for the air-conditioned café or into the other monuments that were still open to the public. Simone had explored some of them before it became too hot.

Although she had Nazaari blood and the Australian climate should have prepared her, she found the baking heat of the desert more of a challenge than she'd anticipated. She decided to freshen up at the restroom alongside the café, then have a cold drink before resuming her study of the sheikh's party. This time she would try to keep her mind on her mission, she promised herself.

The most pressing was to find her father's half brother who'd stayed in Nazaar when her parents had fled to Australia after her father's life was threatened for writing editorials supporting Markaz's father, Kemal. Ali al Hasa had agreed with the old sheikh's efforts to drag Nazaar into the twentieth century, but Kemal had been assassinated for his efforts, along with his older son, forcing Markaz to return from living in America and take over the reins.

Her other purpose was to source new designs and materials for her thriving, Internet-based heirloom embroidery business. Her mother, a skilled seamstress, had stimulated Simone's fascination with Middle Eastern crafts. She'd allowed herself a week to track down Yusef, and another to focus on her business, but the first week was almost up and this was as far as she'd come.

Simone stopped long enough to remove her sun visor and fan herself with it, for all the good it did. Before leaving Australia she'd had her heavy curtain of pale gold hair cut to chin length. Now the strands curled damply in the heat. Her father had teased her mother about their only daughter's golden coloring. Fortunately her features left her parentage in no doubt. Her nose and chin were as well defined as her father's, while her long lashes and full lips were inherited from Sara. She also had Ali's energy and commitment, demonstrated in the success of her business.

In Australia he'd changed their family name from al Hasa to Hayes, settling at Port Lincoln on the fringe of Australia's great desert, the Nullarbor Plain, the landscape most like his homeland. There Ali had started an Arabic newsletter for expatriates. Simone had worked with him for a few years, polishing her language skills, although they still left a lot to be desired in her opinion. When he'd taken the newsletter online, she'd decided it was time to do her own thing, also using the Internet. Ali had been her strongest supporter.

Sadness yawned inside her for her father, brought back no doubt by being surrounded by men who reminded her so much of him. After everything Ali and Sara had gone through making a new life for themselves and their daughter, the ultimate cruelty had been having his life ended by a hit-and-run driver. By his side as she usually was, Sara had suffered a broken leg and bruising, but had recovered.

While Sara's physical injuries had healed, her mind had been slower to recover. She had plunged into a clinical depression that nothing so far had been able to relieve. Thinking of her in the nursing home in Port Lincoln, Simone felt another wave of sadness sweep over her. She hadn't wanted to leave her mother in her present condition, but Sara was in good hands and had begged Simone to find out what had happened to the young relative they'd left behind in Nazaar. Yusef al Hasa would be almost fifty now, no longer the young hothead her mother remembered. At twenty-eight, Simone herself was older than Yusef had been when her parents left Nazaar. They'd wanted him to come with them, but he'd joined the rebels opposing the reform process.

How had he made the leap from rebel to sheikh's guard, Simone wondered. Had he finally been convinced that

Markaz's father was right in wanting to give his people more freedom, especially the women? Or had Yusef simply grown weary of fighting a losing battle?

Nazaar was still far from being a free country, but from her parents Simone knew things had improved greatly in the last thirty years. Women were no longer considered the property of men, and could drive cars and pursue careers, although from what Simone had seen, more than a few men still regarded their wives as possessions. About half the women she'd seen still wore traditional abayas, long black hooded cloaks over their clothes. A very few wore burkas, fabric masks that left only their eyes visible to the world.

The sheikh still ruled, but members of his advisory council were elected by the people every four years. Since Nazaar opened its borders to tourists ten years before, her parents had talked of returning for a visit, but had never gotten around to it. Simone suspected they had preferred to keep their memories intact.

Lost in thought, she was almost bowled over by a woman pushing past her into the ladies' room. "You're excused," she muttered in mild annoyance as she followed the woman into the cool interior. A swinging door leading to the cubicles explained the woman's haste.

Like the rest of the site, the restroom was spotless and gleaming, the rose-colored marble walls in keeping with the historic locale. Wide velvet-covered couches with elaborate curling ends lined the walls and a counter held a brass drinking water fountain and disposable cups. Simone made a beeline for it, slaking her thirst with a sigh of pleasure.

At a basin, she splashed water onto her face and wrists and the back of her neck, glad to have the room to herself for a few seconds. Behind her, a rush of water preceded the other woman's return. Only then, Simone noticed the woman was chalk-white and gripping the edge of the door for support.

Her previous irritation at the woman turned to concern. "Are you all right?"

The woman shook her head, then said in American-accented English, "The heat is affecting me."

"Maybe you should sit down," Simone said, wondering if she should find someone to help. The woman looked really ill.

The woman lurched to one of the couches and dropped onto it, resting her head back against the marble wall. Without asking, Simone filled another cup with water and offered it to her.

Her reward was a shaky smile. "Thanks." She drank quickly, but when she lowered her hand, the cup slid out of her grasp.

Simone picked it up. She had the nagging feeling she'd seen the woman somewhere before. But where and when? Her speech was American, and she had the put-together look of a professional woman. She wore tailored navy pants and a long-sleeved white shirt with the kind of easy elegance Simone envied. The woman would have been attractive but for her waxy skin and the way her short-cropped dark hair was sticking to her face.

Annoyed at feeling helpless, Simone looked around. Fine time for the attendant to be on a break. "Shall I find a doctor for you?"

"No, thanks. I just need to get back to my car."

Suddenly she bent forward, clutching her stomach. She didn't moan, but her tightly compressed lips suggested she wanted to. Alarmed, Simone said, "You're in no condition to drive. I'll find someone who works here to help you."

"No." The command rang with unexpected authority as the woman straightened: "Please don't," she added in an obvious effort to soften the command.

Stayed at the entrance, Simone turned back. "You could have food poisoning, or some kind of bug. You need a doctor."

The woman smiled wanly. "I'll see someone as soon as I get back to my hotel. My car is in the closest parking lot." She levered herself to her feet, but tottered when she took a few steps.

Simone was at her side instantly. "At least let me help you as far as the parking lot."

As they stepped out into the heat the woman's breath caught but she steadied herself. Simone steered her to the blue rental car she indicated, noting that it took the woman three tries to get the doors unlocked with the remote. How on earth did she expect to drive anywhere? "Look, there's a first-aid center near the restroom. Why don't I—"

The woman placed a clammy hand on her arm. "Please don't. There's too much at stake." Too much of what? Sounding as if the effort cost her, she said, "I'm not…I can't…explain any more. But I need you to give something to Markaz." She fumbled in her bag.

Was the woman delirious? "He's surrounded by guards. I couldn't even get close," Simone protested.

"You must, please. His life is at stake."

What had Simone gotten herself into? She hadn't been able to get close enough to the sheikh's party to look for her half uncle. Now she was supposed to take a message to the sheikh from a woman who was either ill or delusional, possibly both.

"You need a doctor," she tried again, adding in desperation, "Why don't I drive you back to your hotel?"

Arriving in a cab, Simone had no car of her own to worry about.

The woman clenched her teeth, but not before Simone had seen them chattering. "I'm not crazy. Tell Markaz you met Natalie. Give him…oh, God, he's coming." She wrenched a ring off the third finger of her right hand and closed Simone's fingers around it, then gave her a shove that almost knocked her off her feet. "He mustn't see you with me. Go."

Regaining her balance, Simone looked in the direction of Natalie's wild-eyed gaze. The only other person nearby was a stocky, dark-haired man in a business suit and reflective sunglasses, weaving his way between the cars. He stopped and spoke to a woman seated in another car. Nothing in his actions seemed to justify Natalie's panic.

Simone debated taking Natalie's keys away from her, but was daunted by the strength she'd felt in that shove. If the woman was demented by the heat or illness, she might become even more violent. Simone reached a sudden decision. "I'm getting help whether you want it or not." She didn't wait for more arguments, as she set off across the parking lot in the direction of a first-aid center she'd passed earlier.

She was almost there when she heard a distant cry and swung around. The man in the business suit was standing over Natalie.

Simone froze. Was the man Natalie's husband, taking care of her at last? But she'd sounded terrified when she'd said, "He's coming." Then the man pushed Natalie into the car and slammed the door.

Before Simone had the thought fully hatched, she was racing toward the car. The man looked up. Seeing her, he sprinted around the car and wrenched open the driver's door and threw himself inside. Seconds later the engine roared into life.

The car was moving by the time she reached it. Futilely she hammered on the window as it slid past her. Natalie was slumped in the seat, but opened her eyes at the sound. Was it Simone's imagination or did she mouth the word *Markaz* before the car picked up speed?

Jumping clear seconds before being run down, Simone could only watch as they sped off, her sense of despair growing. She should have done more to help. But what?

Becoming aware of metal biting into her palm, Simone unclenched her fist and looked at the ring the woman had pressed on her. The gold was incised with symbols, among them a beaver holding a piece of wood. On the shank was a design of two men and a lamp. Nothing that explained what Simone had just witnessed.

Unless the ring meant something to the sheikh.

Outside the main building, a flurry of activity told her he was emerging. The crowd was several people deep, but desperation enabled her to push her way to the front and grab the arm of the nearest guard. "You must help me. A woman's been abducted in the parking lot."

"Report this to Al-Qasr's own security," the guard responded in guttural English. "I cannot leave my post."

"I don't want you to leave your post." *You muscle-bound moron,* she barely resisted adding. "You must tell the sheikh that Natalie needs help urgently. She sent him this."

The guard looked at the ring as if it could bite. "Gifts should be sent to the palace."

"It isn't a gift, it's a message. The sheikh knows the woman who sent it. She needs his help."

The man's determination wavered, but only for a

second, before his jaw hardened and he gestured Simone back. "Take this to local security."

A scattering of applause greeted the appearance of Sheikh Markaz, once again shadowed by his giant bodyguard. What would happen if she threw the ring to the sheikh and called out, "catch"? A vision of being tackled by the giant, her bones breaking under the impact, stopped her.

But she wasn't defeated yet. She reached over the cordon and tugged at the guard's sleeve. "You must give this to His Highness. A woman's life is at stake."

The guard roared a response in Arabic. "Persist and you will find yourself under arrest," he said in English.

Having already considered the possibility, she felt chilled, but her determination notched higher. "The woman told me the sheikh's life is in danger, as well."

That got the guard's attention, she saw, but his barked command also had his colleagues lifting their weapons. The ring glinted in the sunlight as she raised her hands instinctively. "I'm not the threat, but Natalie knows who is. You must find her."

The ruckus she was causing was getting her noticed, she saw, feeling color surge into her face. Suddenly a sensation as if she was caught in the beam of a powerful light dragged her gaze past the guard and she found herself looking into the eyes of Sheikh Markaz himself.

His face appeared to be carved from the same living stone as the monuments around them. His eyes were as dark as the rest of his features, she noticed immediately. Not so much black as the green of a deep ocean cavern. The cavern impression was echoed in the hollows and hard planes of his cheeks, and a faintly cleft jaw that looked like stubbornness personified.

A flare of blatantly masculine interest suddenly lit his gaze, catching her unawares. She hadn't reached her present age without attracting her share of male notice, and she was definitely attracting it now, she realized in amazement. Worse, it wasn't one-sided. Her pulse was double-timing and all he'd done was look her way.

The extraordinary sensation of communion between them was over in an instant, then the sheikh's attention was claimed by the giant. But she was left feeling thunderstruck. What on earth had just happened?

What had happened was he was moving on flanked by his goons, and she was still clutching the ring, she thought, cursing herself for her lapse. He was the richest and most powerful man in the country. That high-voltage look was probably part of his normal arsenal, hardly personal.

The royal party was heading for the luncheon laid on after the inspection, she noted. Access would be strictly controlled, but there must be some way she could get the ring to him, even if she had to slip it onto a tray of drinks being carried into the marquee.

Catching a movement out of the corner of her eye, she froze. A man in a business suit was making a beeline for her through the crowd.

As Markaz bin Kemal al Nazaari came down the steps of Al-Qasr's main monument, he lifted his hand in the not-quite wave that acknowledged the crowd's good wishes, but conserved his energy. The cheers gratified him. Not everyone in Nazaar felt kindly toward his government. The rebels were in a minority, but a troublesome one. And sometimes dangerous. Already today, he'd been informed of a bomb threat that had closed Raisa International Airport.

A commotion in the crowd had him bracing himself. Was the airport incident a diversion for an attempt on his life here? But his bodyguard Fayed remained relaxed as he leaned closer. "It seems you've caught the eye of a pretty tourist, Markaz," he murmured for the sheikh's ears alone.

Markaz felt his mouth curve. He and Fayed had grown up together, as close as brothers, and Markaz trusted the big man with his life. He sought out the source of the fuss, then felt something inside him catch. "I could do worse."

"Indeed you could, my friend. She's beautiful."

Beautiful was too mundane a description, Markaz thought. Engaged in an altercation with a guard, the woman's eyes flashed blue-green like the oasis at the sheikh's desert lodge. Under a tinted sun visor, her short golden hair feathered around her animated face, her strong features and golden coloring also speaking of the desert. Who was she and where was she from, this exotic melding of east and west?

By tourist standards she was modestly dressed in an embroidered white peasant blouse gathered decorously at the neck and with long sleeves. The diaphanous fabric hinted at small, high breasts and a neat waist. He couldn't see her legs beneath a flowing wine-colored skirt, but if they were as shapely as the rest of her…

Suddenly she looked straight into his eyes, fantasy made flesh. He felt the effect all the way to his groin, and his breath strangled. But she was more than sexy. She had fire. She reminded him of an Arab thoroughbred. Probably untamable, but an adventure to attempt.

Fayed chuckled. "This must be love. She's come prepared with a ring."

The flash of gold in her palm made Markaz blink. His

people often tried to press gifts and flowers upon their sheikh, although not usually the tourists, and a ring was a novelty. A flick of his fingers brought Fayed's head closer. "Find out what she wants."

If he'd surprised his friend, Fayed was too disciplined to show it. "As you wish. Do you want her brought to you?"

Markaz's power extended that far, but he shook his head. "Not in the way you're thinking, my salacious friend. She looks troubled. Perhaps I can help."

"And if it is love?"

"Then tell her diplomatically that my country has first claim on my heart."

Fayed frowned. "No country can satisfy all of a man's desires."

This woman could. Markaz dismissed the thought as fast as it arose. Not so easily dismissed was the aching conviction that Fayed was right.

Chapter 2

Driven by a feeling of urgency she didn't stop to question, Simone shoved the ring into her skirt pocket and plunged into the heart of the crowd, keeping her head down. The man looking for her was the same one who'd forced the American woman into her car, she was certain. Now he was after Simone.

Only when the crowd around her thinned out did Simone realize her pursuer had steered her away from the security of the throng toward a narrow alleyway. Footsteps pounding ever closer left her little choice but to head down the alley and hope it took her back to a more populous part of the ruins.

The buildings threw strange shadows and the unreadable inscriptions over the doors of the ancient houses made navigation challenging. She had no idea where the alley led and she couldn't risk stopping to ask for directions.

The man was gaining on her as she ducked under an

archway and across a courtyard into yet another alleyway on the opposite side. She was among the tombs now, she recognized from her earlier explorations. According to the guidebook, the houses had belonged to priests, embalmers and other workers in the funerary trade when most of Al-Qasr had functioned as a gigantic mausoleum for a long-dead civilization. No one had been buried here for millennia.

Hoping she wouldn't be the exception, she plunged through a passage so narrow she could easily touch both sides. Then she emerged into an unrestored part of Al-Qasr, where fallen stones were piled haphazardly, although glimpses of intricate carving could still be seen. A notice in several languages warned her that this area was not open to visitors and was unsafe. Tell her something she didn't know.

Chest heaving with exertion, she stopped long enough to see there was no refuge in sight. She needed to reach a more crowded area. And to spend a lot more time in the gym after she got home to Australia. If she got home.

Her parents had outwitted their enemies so the family could live without fear in another country. Simone wasn't letting their sacrifice count for nothing by dying in Nazaar at the hands of some lowlife. She had no idea who her pursuer was or what he wanted, although it seemed likely he wanted to find out what Natalie had told her. Did the ring carry a message? Should Simone hide it or throw it away?

No time to do either. She saw the business-suited man appear in the unrestored area so she charged on, jamming her elbow against her side to relieve a stitch. Hearing the sounds of commerce somewhere to her right, she shot down yet another alleyway only to find herself facing a towering wall of sandstone.

A fissure like the eye of a needle opened to the left and she forced her way through it, hoping Business Suit was too bulky to follow. Popping out of the fissure, she looked wildly to right and left. Which way now? Then a hand grasped the back of her shirt and her feet dangled in air as she was lifted off the ground.

She fought back using moves she'd only practiced in her martial arts classes. It wasn't supposed to matter that her captor was twice her size. It wasn't Business Suit she saw, blinking to clear the sweat from her eyes. This attacker was bearded and wore a white dishdasha. An accomplice? Had she been herded into a trap?

Not waiting for an introduction, she brought her knee up to impact where it could do the most damage. The big man grunted in pain and doubled over, but he didn't let go. One of the dinosaur types who took a while for messages to travel from their lumbering bodies to their tiny brains, she thought, aiming for his eyes with her stiffened fingers. He straightened and held her at arm's length so her punches landed in air.

Muttering something in Arabic that didn't sound repeatable, he flipped her around and slammed her against a wall, driving the air out of her body. Before she could regroup, her arms were yanked high up behind her back and her wrists cuffed in one beefy hand.

"Now will you be still?" he demanded in accented English.

"Go to hell," she snarled, struggling.

"Whatever Sheikh Markaz saw in you, I hope it's worth it," the big man said, the statement sounding like a curse.

Confused, Simone stopped fighting. "You're with the *sheikh?*"

"I am Fayed, his personal bodyguard. He sent me to

find out what need was so pressing you'd risk arrest to reach him."

She was still eating sandstone, and he hadn't released his punishing grip on her arms. She'd been too busy resisting to recognize the giant who'd been glued to the sheikh's side. "Let me go and I might tell you."

"I want your word you will not attack me again or try to run away."

"I'll behave," she said resignedly. A painful jerk on her arms told her this wasn't good enough. "All right, I promise."

The pressure on her abused shoulders eased as he released her. She grimaced and rubbed her upper arms with her crossed hands. "Did the sheikh tell you to rough me up?"

The massive man frowned. "He gave no such order. I only did so because you attacked me first."

Her gaze acknowledged their relative sizes. "Your boss might find that hard to believe."

"As do I," Fayed said in his rumbling basso profundo voice. His pained expression and the careful way he moved made her think she'd damaged more than his pride.

Remembering her pursuer, she looked around nervously.

Fayed caught the look. "What is it?"

"There's a man following me. I think he wants this."

She fished in her pocket and pulled out the ring. Fayed's eyes widened at the sight. "Where did you get that?"

"From a woman called Natalie. She asked me to give it to the sheikh." Fayed reached for the ring, but Simone closed her fingers around it. "Uh-uh. If I give it to you now, you might abandon me to Business Suit."

"Business Suit?"

"The man following me. He must have seen Natalie give me the ring."

"Who are you?"

She had a feeling he didn't want her life story. "Simone Hayes, from Australia."

Fayed took her arm. "Come with me, Simone Hayes."

"I'd rather take you to where I last saw Natalie."

"My orders are to learn what you require. I am not leaving the sheikh alone any longer to go on a wild-goose chase on your behalf."

"Even if the wild-goose chase is what I require?"

"We'll let Sheikh Markaz be the judge."

In the meantime, anything could be happening to Natalie. Held fast in the giant's grip, Simone could only hope that she'd distracted Business Suit long enough to let the other woman get away.

Not sure if she should feel reassured to be in the company of a man built like a tank, or worried that he might be escorting her deeper into trouble, she had little choice but to trot at his side, taking two steps to every one of his.

They were almost back at the main monument where a group of officials, the sheikh an imposing figure in their midst, clustered beside the royal marquee. She must have been running in circles. "Do you know what the ring means?" she asked, gulping air.

Fayed wasn't even breathing hard. "Sheikh Markaz will tell you what he wishes you to know."

Remembering the electrifying look the sheikh had given her when their eyes met for the merest moment, she balked. He was the ruler of the whole country. She didn't want to meet him looking as if she'd been dragged through a hedge. Not because of any feminine need to dazzle him, but because she didn't want to give him a bad impression of Australian womanhood. Or so she told herself. "At least give me a few seconds to make myself presentable."

"You will not cause any more trouble." It wasn't a question.

"Considering that my options comprise going with you, or dealing with Natalie's attacker, I don't have much choice."

"Good."

Crazy though it seemed, she was warming to this mountain of a man. His voice might sound like the earth itself opening up, and he had strange ideas of how to treat a lady, but his devotion to the sheikh was encouraging. Fayed would keep her safe for as long as his boss wished it.

The bodyguard steered her into a shaded area between two columns, but didn't take his eyes off her as she brushed sand off her clothing and tucked her blouse back into her skirt. The sun visor was lost among the ruins, but she carried her shoulder bag slung across her body, so her purse had survived the ordeal.

Retrieving a comb and compact, she did what she could to tidy her hair, and blotted her streaming face. "Right, let's meet His Highness," she said, hoping she sounded more confident than she felt.

Fayed appropriated her arm again. "You will not make any untoward moves, and you will speak only when the sheikh speaks to you."

She could imagine the outcome if she made any move Fayed interpreted as threatening to his boss. "Count on it."

The moment's respite had allowed her to catch her breath so she wasn't panting too obviously when Fayed led her to where the sheikh was holding court. She'd hate him to think she was breathing heavily on his account.

Fayed carved his way through the group until he reached the sheikh's side where he made a salaam, the graceful hand gesture encompassing head and heart accompanied by a bow from the neck. "Your Highness, this is Simone Hayes, from Australia. I think you will be interested in what she has to say."

He bent and whispered a few words in the sheikh's ear, too low for Simone to hear. It was enough to bring a look of anger to the sheikh's face, and he snapped out what sounded like an instruction in return. She saw Fayed nod then approach a pair of the sheikh's soldiers and speak to them in turn.

The moment Fayed brought Simone Hayes to Markaz, he had the renewed sense of electricity arcing between them, as if she were more than an overexcited tourist who'd disrupted his inspection. He told himself he'd had a long morning dealing with his normal duties, the bomb threat at the airport, and now this visit. He was tired. He should have left Simone to the guards instead of sending Fayed after her.

But he owed the man his life a couple of times over, and trusted his judgment. What Fayed had already told the sheikh had shaken him. If his friend believed Simone's story was worth hearing, then it was.

"Excuse us for a few moments," he said now to the director of Al-Qasr, who'd been telling him more about the restoration work. The man regarded her curiously, but salaamed and moved away to join another group, leaving the sheikh and Simone in a small island of clear space.

Markaz was aware of Fayed returning to his side.

"Would you get Miss Hayes a drink?" the sheikh asked him. "Coffee or something cold?"

Simone brushed a hand across her brow. "Cold, thank you."

Fayed gestured to a passing waiter, who presented a tray of ice-frosted glasses to her with alacrity. The young woman accepted some sparkling water and drank half of it right away. Markaz felt a flash of envy for the straw between her parted lips. Such beautiful lips, sensuously full and rosy without any sign of artificial enhancement.

In an effort to stop staring at her mouth, he drained the bitter coffee in his thimble-sized cup, passing his hand over it to stop the waiter refilling it. He'd already drunk two cups out of politeness.

The woman lifted her head and smiled at him, her sea-foam eyes brilliant. "Thank you, Your Highness, I was thirsty," she said, earning a frown from Fayed.

Sometimes his bodyguard was more of a stickler for protocol than Markaz himself, he thought. "Even at this time of year, the heat can be challenging if you're not accustomed to it."

She nodded. "Coming from Australia I should be, but I hadn't planned on being chased all over Al-Qasr."

The sheikh's surprised look went to his bodyguard. His orders hadn't extended to hounding her. "By Fayed?"

"No, by another man. Fayed rescued me from him."

The gingerly way his friend was moving suggested there was more to the story, but now wasn't the time to go into details. He would get them from Fayed later. "Who was chasing you?"

She cast a nervous glance around as if her pursuer might still be in the vicinity. "The man I saw abducting Natalie."

At hearing his ex-wife's name from this woman's lips,

slivers of ice pierced Markaz. Fayed had already told him she had been seen here, and he had dispatched men to investigate at Markaz's request. Suddenly the ring Simone had tried to pass to him over the barricades assumed a more sinister importance. Could it contain the information he'd been told Natalie would deliver to him at Al-Qasr?

He masked his concern. "What is your involvement with Natalie?"

"She was feeling ill so I helped her back to the parking lot. As I was leaving her, I saw a man force her into the car. I tried to help, but he got away. I decided to approach you."

He felt his gaze harden. "How did you know to come to me?"

"Natalie said your life was in danger, and gave me this for you." Shifting the glass to her left hand, she fumbled in the pocket of her skirt.

But the sheikh closed his hand over hers. "Not here. Join us for lunch inside the marquee."

Simone's hand was still in her pocket, but the sheikh's touch seemed to burn through the light fabric of her skirt. She was imagining it, just as she'd imagined his gaze fixated on her mouth, she assured herself.

She took her hand out of her pocket and pressed the palm against her thigh. "I'm hardly dressed for this company."

He took her hand and lifted it close to his mouth, his lips whispering over the back of it. "You would be an ornament to any occasion just as you are."

In a flash she worked out what he was doing. Sheikh Markhaz was reputed to have a roving eye. He certainly didn't remain with any one woman for long. He was creating the impression that Simone had attracted his interest, so no one would be surprised if he kept her at his side.

Knowing his attention was an act didn't stop her pulse from racing. It was all she could do not to rub the back of her hand where his courtly kiss had scorched her like a flame. "As Your Highness wishes."

"My name is Markaz," he murmured.

If Fayed had disapproved of her speaking to Markaz unbidden, at this he looked thunderstruck. Men and women mixed more freely in Nazaar than in many Arabian countries, but behavior was still conservative by Western standards. The sheikh could have called her Miss Simone without raising eyebrows, but inviting her to use his first name so quickly was a scandalous intimacy.

Was it? She'd been so sure he was putting on an act that she hadn't let herself think what would happen if there was more to it. He was certainly the most attractive man she'd met in a long time. And she'd broken up with Nick a couple of months before leaving Australia, so there was no man in her life, either.

Stop this, she instructed herself before the fantasy could get any more out of hand. The sheikh had invited her to an official lunch, presumably so she could tell him what she'd seen away from public view. It was hardly an invitation to join his harem.

"I'd feel happier if you'd send someone to look for Natalie," she said, feeling guilty for indulging in stupid daydreams while the other woman was in danger.

The sheikh looked grim. "It is already being done. As soon as Fayed told me she was here, I dispatched men to investigate. As of yet she has not been located."

Now Simone understood the significance of his discussion with Fayed. "Her car was parked directly across from the entrance to the north parking lot. She was driving a dark blue coupe with rental plates. I didn't get the number."

Markaz's gesture brought Fayed closer. Their Arabic was too soft for her to translate, although she hoped he was giving Fayed the extra information. The big man once more melted into the crowd.

"If Natalie is in the area, Fayed will find her," Markaz said.

"You didn't ask me what she looks like."

"We already know. The item she gave you could only have come from my ex-wife."

Suddenly Simone knew why Natalie had seemed familiar. She was the woman he'd married in America, and divorced soon after becoming sheikh. Photos of them together had been on the Web sites Simone had researched for her trip, but Natalie had changed enough in ten years to stop Simone from recognizing her.

She barely had time to absorb this information before Markaz led her into the marquee where long, low tables were covered by dazzling white cloths and more delicacies than Simone had seen in a department store food hall.

At the head of the official table, Markaz's chair had a higher back than the others, gilded and padded in wine-colored brocade. At his insistence she seated herself at his right, aware of causing a flurry of rearrangements. Although the Al-Qasr staff tried to be unobtrusive about accommodating her, Simone's presence had undoubtedly caused a stir.

Enormous platters of crepelike bread, mounds of glistening rice and fragrant lamb, smoked chicken, stuffed grape leaves, marrow and squash and salads were served.

Simone heard almost no conversation not related to the magnificence of the feast, but she didn't find this unusual. To the end of his days her father had never become comfortable with the Western habit of conversing over a meal. He'd preferred small talk to take place over coffee and tea before and after a meal.

"You are hardly eating," Markaz observed. "If you don't wish to offend our hosts, you should taste a little of everything."

Natalie's ring was burning a hole in her pocket, but she followed the sheikh's lead and paid attention to the feast. Knowing that Fayed was searching for Natalie had eased Simone's mind enough so she could absorb her surroundings. Unfortunately the royal guards hadn't accompanied the guests into the marquee and would most likely be eating elsewhere. So she couldn't use the opportunity to look for Yusef al Hasa.

However bizarre the circumstances, she was a guest of Sheikh Markaz bin Kemal al Nazaari, she reminded herself, picturing her mother's response when she heard. Would it be enough to pierce Sara's depression? Simone hoped so, because unless she located Yusef among the sheikh's escort after the meal, she doubted she'd get a chance like this again.

Moving lightly for such a big man, Fayed appeared at his boss's shoulder. Simone didn't need to hear what was said to know the news wasn't encouraging. Fayed's expression was grim. He didn't like disappointing the sheikh, she concluded. She doubted it was because Markaz was a demanding boss. He would be tough but fair, she assessed, having noted his courteous treatment of those assigned to serve him.

How had he come to marry an American, she wondered.

Not that his personal life was any of her business. She was naturally curious. And why did his ex-wife want him to watch his back? The antiroyal forces in Nazaar were far less of a problem than in her parents' time, or Simone would never have chosen to visit. Were they on the rise again as Markaz steered the country closer to full democracy?

He leaned toward her. "A short time ago the guards at the entrance to Al-Qasr observed a dark blue rental car speeding away with a man at the wheel and a woman apparently asleep in the passenger seat."

Simone's tension notched higher. "Natalie and Business Suit."

He inclined his head. "Evidently."

She pulled out the ring and pressed it into his hand beneath the table. "She wanted me to give you this."

Recognition came swiftly. "It's our class ring from Harvard. To alumni, the beaver is known as the brass rat." He showed her a matching ring on his right hand.

Her disappointment showed. "Then the ring isn't a message?"

He hesitated long enough to suggest that there was more to the ring than he was prepared to share with her. After being chased through the ruins with the item in her possession, she wasn't sure she wanted to know.

"The design is modified to reflect each class's spirit and experiences. By sending our class ring, Natalie made sure her identity is in no doubt," he said.

"Business Suit appeared before she could tell me any more, other than that your life is in danger."

"As yours may well be now."

Her startled gaze lifted to his. "But Fayed said the man left."

"His people will want to know how much Natalie told you, and what you have shared with me. You should not return to your hotel tonight."

This was more than she'd bargained for. "My bags are there and my passport's in the hotel safe. Could you arrange their return, if I check in to another hotel?"

He looked amused and she had to remind herself of who and what he was. In Nazaar, he could do anything he wished. "One hotel is as risky as another."

"Then where—"

He didn't wait for her to finish. "Ideally I would have you placed on a flight home to Australia for your safety. But the airport is closed due to a bomb scare. Flights won't be back to normal until tomorrow."

She lifted her head. "In any case, I can't leave yet. I have…business appointments," she finished, knowing the explanation sounded lame. Instinct told her not to mention Yusef to the sheikh. He might not be so kindly disposed toward her if he knew she hoped to contact a former rebel. And she hadn't come all this way to be packed off home without achieving her goal.

"No business appointment is worth your life."

"You're not leaving," she pointed out, adding belatedly, "Your Highness."

His wry smile acknowledged the title. "In my position, danger is a part of life. However, the influence of the rebels is waning. They are the ones fighting for their lives now."

"Desperate people have been known to do desperate things."

"True, and you have attracted their attention."

She spread her hands wide. "What can I do?"

"Return with my party to the palace at Raisa where you

will be under royal protection until it is safe for you to leave the country."

Excitement bubbled through her, warring with an awareness of danger. She told herself she was excited because her chances of finding Yusef among the royal guard had greatly improved. Not because she would be spending more time around Markaz. "I appreciate the offer," she said.

Again that maddening half smile played around his sensuous mouth, as if she were a child he was indulging. "You may consider it an offer if you wish."

As long as she did as he commanded, she read between the lines, her hackles rising. She disliked being ordered around. But if the rebels had Natalie, Simone didn't plan on being their next victim. There was only one possible response. "Thank you. I accept your offer."

Chapter 3

Markaz kept her at his side as they made their way back to the waiting fleet of cars. If the situation hadn't been so nerve-racking, she would have enjoyed the ripples her appearance with the sheikh caused among the onlookers.

There were advantages to being under royal protection, she decided. Not only did she feel less vulnerable having Markaz's guards around her, she felt like a celebrity. Unlike back home, there'd be no tabloid headlines speculating about the sheikh's mystery woman tomorrow. Nazaar might be edging toward democracy, but the media still treated the royal family with deference.

She had expected to ride in one of the following cars with members of the sheikh's entourage, but Markaz indicated she was to ride with him in the vehicle flying the royal standard. As they approached, a driver opened the door for them and Markaz gestured for her to get in. She hesitated. "Are you sure this is a good idea?"

"Are you worried about your image or mine?" he asked dryly. Before she could answer, he added, "It's a little late to trouble yourself about either one. The gossip mills will already be working overtime."

So Nazaar had its version of the tabloids, she thought. Remembering the whispers following her when she'd been the only child with refugee parents in her class at school, she kept her head high. What people chose to say about her was their business. She knew why she was with Markaz, and if being with him kept her safe and got her closer to her goal of finding Yusef, she could handle the gossip. It wasn't as if he really had a romantic interest in her.

All the same she was aware of how close together they were once the driver closed the car door. There was room enough for her to stretch her legs out, but Markaz seemed to shrink the space alarmingly. While they were standing, Simone hadn't noticed a big difference in their heights, but in the car he seemed so broad and solid that she automatically tucked herself into a corner to give him more space.

Fayed squeezed into the front seat beside the driver, and pressed a button, closing a tinted glass screen to give the passengers privacy. In the enclosed space, her senses were stirred by the faint scent of cinnamon and citrus from the sheikh's cologne. Normally she preferred men who smelled cleanly of soap and talc, but there was something disturbingly sensual about whatever Markaz was wearing.

She wasn't usually attracted to men in skirts, either, she thought. But the traditional robes looked so perfect on him that she couldn't imagine him wearing anything else. Up close, the gold embroidery on his *mishlah* was even more intricate than it had looked from a distance.

The motorcade was gathering speed out of Al-Qasr when he said, "Will you know me again next time you see me?"

She would know him anywhere, came the unbidden thought. He dominated the space in the car as much by force of personality as physical size. Since she could hardly say so, she said, "I didn't mean to stare, but I'm interested in traditional embroidery, and you're wearing a wonderful example."

"You find my *clothes* riveting?" His tone was all wounded male pride.

The alternative was to admit how riveting she found *him,* and she didn't feel any such thing. "My business specializes in heirloom embroidery designs. Nazaar designs are not yet famous, but they should be," she explained.

"Let me guess. You have a mission to bring our traditional crafts to the attention of the Western world?"

His sarcasm wasn't lost on her. "Not so much a mission as a passion."

"Old women have a passion for embroidery. You can't be more than twenty-five."

"Twenty-eight," she corrected, pleased that he thought her younger. "Embroidery is popular with people of all ages. My Internet business even has a few men as customers."

Looking unconvinced, the sheikh opened a compartment to reveal a well-stocked bar. "Champagne?"

She had never drunk champagne in a moving car before. And she found she didn't like having him think of her as stuffy, so she nodded. "I'd love some."

The famous label on the bottle he opened made her blink. But what else would one drink in the back of a Rolls Royce? she thought as he poured two glasses and raised his to her. "*Santé.*"

She returned the toast. "To Your Highness's health."

His dark eyes met hers over the rim of the glass. "I trust we'll both enjoy good health for a long time to come."

Reminded of why she was in his company, Simone's mood darkened and Markaz frowned in response. "I don't mean to blacken your mood."

"Business Suit blackened it when he abducted Natalie, then came after me this morning," she said. "For a few minutes, I allowed myself to forget."

"Then I must find a way to make you forget again. When you spoke of your passion for embroidery, you looked even more vibrant and beautiful."

She managed a slight smile. She wasn't beautiful, but a little flattery never hurt. "How do you stand being under threat as part of your everyday existence?"

He shrugged. "Everyone is under some kind of threat, whether it's from illness, misfortune or the passage of time. Being royal simply makes one more conscious of life's hazards."

She sipped champagne. "I hadn't thought about it like that. But you can't equate getting sick or old with the threat of assassination."

A flicking gesture of his fingers dismissed her argument, but her smile was teasing as he said, "I am the sheikh. I can do anything I choose."

Not sure why, she felt driven to be contrary. "Your power must have some limits. Surely you can't command the weather, or make someone fall in love with you?" Now why had she chosen that example?

He didn't seem fazed. "Are you sure?"

"About the weather?"

Leaning forward, he fingered pads on a control panel. Instantly, the air around her became much cooler. "What is air-conditioning but controlling the weather? As to your second example?"

Despite the chill air sliding over her skin, she felt over-heated suddenly. The champagne must be having an effect. "Yes?"

"I would not want to make someone fall in love with me. Love is overrated as a means of choosing a life part-ner."

Was he speaking as a man who'd been once bitten? "I wouldn't know."

He toyed with the stem of his glass. "You can't tell me that someone as attractive as you has never been in love?"

Two compliments in one conversation. She'd have to be careful she didn't start believing him. She paid attention to the walnut grove they were driving through. In contrast to the soaring sandstone hills locking in Al-Qasr, the surrounding region was green and fertile, dotted with villages where time appeared to have stood still. She turned back to the sheikh. "I thought I was in love until recently. It didn't work out."

He smiled in satisfaction. "See? You bear out my thesis that love is overrated."

"Just because one relationship goes sour doesn't mean the whole notion is a crock."

"Then you are a romantic fool."

She shifted sideways, the buttery-soft leather tilting her closer to him. "You're the boss, Your Highness."

Without asking, he topped up her champagne glass. "If I thought you meant that, I'd be disappointed."

She lifted the glass and studied the bubbling liquid, then lowered it slowly. "Then with respect, Your Highness, you're dead wrong. I may be a romantic, but I don't think I'm a fool."

"No," he said after a pause, "I don't think so, either."

"Thank you."

His low laugh rippled through her like a caress. "Didn't you expect me to concede the point?"

She dragged her free hand through her hair. "After this crazy day, I don't know what I expect anymore. This morning I was an ordinary visitor. Now I'm the target of a criminal, forced to hide out in a royal palace."

His gesture took in their luxurious surroundings. "Is it such a troubling prospect?"

"If I said yes, I would be a fool. This is a once-in-a-life-time experience." Afraid the champagne was starting to affect her, she put her unfinished glass down on the bar. "I only wish I were here under less harrowing circumstances."

"The police are already at work tracking down Natalie's car. Her assailant will not be a threat to you for long," he assured her.

Their bodies were so close. Another couple of inches and she'd be touching him. She held herself rigid, aware of the champagne working to undermine her self-control. "I was thinking of the threat to you."

His gaze skimmed over her face. "You aren't a fool, Simone Hayes. But you are a dreamer."

He made it sound like a flaw. "Because I don't want to see you hurt?"

Her concern had touched him, she saw as his gaze softened. "I didn't mean it as a criticism. Dreams are the first steps to making the world better. But you should be dreaming on your own account, not on mine."

"Can't I do both?"

The car rounded a curve, sliding her farther into his personal space. The contact was momentary before she pulled back, but the effect lingered. He fascinated her for all the wrong reasons. Concern for his safety only went so far.

She was still pondering the problem when the motorcade approached the massive wrought-iron gates guarding the entrance to the Raisa Palace. She had already seen the complex from her hotel. Indeed it was hard to miss. Situated on a massive rocky spur overlooking the city, the palace had the stark simplicity of a fortress and dominated the road linking Raisa to Al-Qasr and the desert beyond. Terraced gardens surrounded the palace, while more gardens planted with cypress groves decorated the park within the gates and around the buildings. She had read about the palace, but never expected to be a guest here. "It's hard to believe this is a private home."

"It also serves as the administrative heart of the kingdom," he explained. "We are passing Dar el Baranie, the exterior lodging. Next is Dar el Wousta, the middle lodging. My true home is Dar el Harem, the private quarters."

Here Markaz's motorcade glided to a halt under an elegant arcade. The facade of this building was adorned with delicate sculptures and wonderful carved marble and alcoves. As the driver opened the door for them and staff hurried to assist them, she felt as if she were stepping into the pages of a fairy tale.

Markaz's pleasure in his home was magnified by seeing it through Simone's eyes. Having grown up in the palace, he was largely immune to the effect, but he enjoyed watching others gain their first glimpse of royal life. Simone's evident appreciation was especially satisfying.

Seldom had anyone shown as much selfless concern for him as she'd done today. She'd risked her life to bring him the ring, without knowing that it contained codes to the operation of a new defensive weapon developed between his country and America for Nazaar's future security. His visit to Al-Qasr had been devised so Natalie could deliver the codes. Only concern for both women's safety had stopped him from telling Simone of the great service she'd done his country. He decided to find a special way to show her his gratitude.

Only a generation ago, the sheikh would have thanked her by taking her to his bed. Just as well she was preoccupied, he thought as an almost painful pleasure bloomed through him. He shifted to ease the sudden pressure in his loins, wondering how she'd react if she knew. Probably violently, and his eyes gleamed at the thought of intercepting her hand on the way to his cheek and crushing her fingers to his lips. She'd be no easy conquest, this curious mix of desert daughter and self-assured Western woman.

Who was Simone Hayes? He looked forward to finding out. Not the practical details his security people would provide for him within hours, but the essence of her that was less easily uncovered. A closer look had affirmed his suspicion that Arab ancestry had sculpted her distinctive features and kissed her flawless skin with gold. But where and how, and was the connection recent or generations ago? And where did her heart belong?

Back in his father's time, the law had allowed the *sheikh of sheikhs* to possess any woman catching his eye. Not that Kemal bin Aziz al Nazaari had ever indulged the privilege, Markaz thought, with the inescapable sense of loss accompanying memories of his father. Kemal had joked about taking more wives, knowing full well that there was only room for one woman in his heart.

Norah Robinson had been an American nurse working

for a royal cousin, when Kemal went to stay with them. After his arm was slashed to the bone while training a new falcon, Norah had tended his injury and captured his heart. Ten years ago a rebel bomb had killed Kemal and their older son, Esan. Norah had carried on magnificently, but Markaz knew his mother still grieved the loss every day.

His parents' example was the reason Markaz had married Natalie so quickly. Wanting what they'd had, he'd assumed it automatically followed physical desire. Even choosing an American wife had been an unconscious wish to replicate his father's happiness. Nowadays Markaz knew better. But by his oath, Simone made him wish the dream had not died with the ending of his marriage.

He watched her until the driver opened the car door, then got out slowly, reluctant to leave their shared cocoon. Usually surrounded by servants and advisors, he treasured his moments of solitude, yet traveling with Simone was better than being alone. It was all he could do not to step back into the car and order the driver to keep going.

At the entrance to Dar el Harem, she'd been greeted by an army of servants. Markaz had assigned a young relative called Amal to look after her, and Simone was pleased with his choice.

In her late twenties, Amal was tall and reed-slim, with hair like black silk reaching to her waist. The unconscious elegance of her movements suggested a dancer's training, unless all members of the royal family moved with such grace.

Simone's professional interest was piqued by the woman's outfit of a long galabia over a pair of loose, flowing trousers known as the *sirwall.* A closer look at the exquisite beadwork on the galabia would have to wait until she'd settled in, Simone thought.

"I always thought a harem was a place of seclusion for women," Simone commented as Amal showed her around the women's quarters. Like most people Simone had encountered in Nazaar, Amal's English was excellent, far better than Simone's Arabic. At this rate she'd have little chance to work on her language skills, but resolved to make the effort.

"The word *harem* describes the living quarters of the sheikh and his family," Amal explained in her soft, musical voice. "Because we women have our own quarters, don't imagine that we're locked away. Some of us wear the abaya—the long cloak—over our clothes in public because we like creating an air of mystique. But we are educated, have careers and personal freedom much like your own. I live in the harem while studying for a degree in social work at Raisa University. These quarters are a sanctuary, not a prison."

"I never thought they were," Simone demurred, although she had been thinking along those lines. Hardly surprising, given the massive doors separating the women's quarters from the rest of the palace, and the guards at the entrance.

Although she studied the guards unobtrusively, none of them fit her mother's description of her father's half brother. Not unexpected, given that the sheikh's staff must number in the hundreds. Finding Yusef was unlikely to be that quick or easy.

She returned her attention to her guide. "Should I address you as Princess, Your Highness, or what?"

Amal smiled. "As a member of the al Nazaari family, technically I am addressed as Princess, but I rarely use a title. I'd like you to call me Amal."

"And I'm Simone," she agreed, feeling as if she'd made a friend in the palace.

"Before he left Al-Qasr, Sheikh Markaz ordered your things brought from your hotel. They have been placed in your room," Amal said.

The room was a gracious blend of East and West, with priceless carpets scattered over the marble floors. The ceilings were finely carved and colored, and arched doorways opened onto a terrace hung with ferns. The canopied bed could have accommodated several people, Simone thought. Her bags looked lost beside it. They were already unpacked, she found when she checked. The staff hadn't wasted any time carrying out the sheikh's orders.

Amal opened another door to reveal a marble-floored reception room and beyond that, a domed bathroom. In the center, framed by columns, was a bathtub as large as a child's wading pool. Simone immediately put a dip at the top of her to do list.

But first she needed to do something else. "Is there a telephone I can use to call my mother in Australia?"

Amal looked surprised at the question. "Of course." Returning to the bedroom, she opened an ornate cabinet to reveal an electronic console and took out a remote control. "I'll translate the settings for you."

"My Arabic isn't as good as your English, but I can read this." Simone laughed. "Knowing how it works is a different matter."

Leaning across her, Amal tapped keys with a long, rose-tipped nail. "This operates the audiovisual system, this the climate controls and these buttons are for the telecommunications system. If you give your mother the number on the handset, she can call you directly or leave voice mail for you. The line is scrambled for security. If you require anything else, call me on the internal system. After you make your phone call to Australia, you'll have time to rest and freshen up before you dine with the sheikh tonight."

This was news to Simone. "I didn't know I'd been invited." How did she feel about spending time with him on his own ground?

Evidently there wasn't a choice. "His Highness will send for you at eight."

Figuring out the high-tech phone system was less of a challenge than talking to her mother. Sara's depression had worsened, her mother's nurse who liked being called simply Mrs. H informed Simone. Sara was under sedation and would be told of her daughter's call when she awoke.

"Should I come home early?" Simone asked.

Down the line, Mrs. H's tone gentled. "At this point, it wouldn't help. We're doing all we can for her. There's nothing more you can do."

Except find her half uncle, Simone thought. No point raising her mother's hopes until she had definite news. Or worrying her by letting her know about Simone's present situation. "Give her my love," she said before hanging up.

She tried to suppress her fear. Mrs. H was a capable professional who was giving her mother the best of care. Worrying wasn't going to change matters. Simone would be better off concentrating on her objective. Right now Markaz was the key.

What did one wear to dine with a sheikh? Her clothes had been chosen for business and sightseeing, but she'd brought a long, slinky black dress with a matching chiffon wrap just in case.

First the tub beckoned. Who could resist such luxury? As water gushed from a swan-shaped gold fountain, she threw in handfuls of scented bath crystals in the shape of rose petals she found in a tall glass jar behind one of the columns. Then she shed her clothes and stepped in. Bliss.

Some time later, feeling refreshed, she swathed herself in a towel the size of a tablecloth, wound another around her freshly washed hair and padded barefoot back to the bedroom. And stopped in surprise.

On the bed, someone had laid out a fabulous peacock-blue jeweled and embroidered galabia and matching *sir-wall* for her. She fingered the fine fabric in delight. Pure silk. The gold-and-silver embroidery and beadwork was finer than anything she'd seen before and she turned it over in her hands, marveling. Wearing this, a woman had to feel like a princess.

Forgetting the nap she'd intended to take, she dug in her cosmetics bag for eye shadow and eyeliner and spent an absorbing half hour experimenting with a look that would do justice to the fabulous clothes.

By the time she was satisfied, she could barely keep her eyes open, and blamed the heat and the stress of the morning at Al-Qasr. She removed her experimental makeup, carefully lifted the gorgeous outfit off the bed and draped it over a chair, then wrapped a robe around herself and stretched out full length. Within minutes she was deeply asleep.

Someone was in her hotel room. Heart pounding, she jerked to full wakefulness and sat up to the realization that this wasn't a hotel. And the intruder was a maid who looked as startled as Simone.

"My apologies for disturbing you," she said softly in Arabic. "I brought tea for you."

"What time is it?" Simone asked in the same language. Almost six in the evening, she was told. She had slept for over two hours. Swinging herself out of bed, she said, "Then it's a good thing you woke me. I'd have slept the clock around otherwise."

On the terrace, the maid had set out hot mint tea, fresh figs, plums, apricots and dates, the shredded pastry stuffed with white cheese called *kanefeh* and tiny pots of creamy bread pudding. Assured that this was more than adequate, the maid left her to her tea.

At this rate she would need more than visits to the gym to balance the indulgences when she returned to Australia. Disciplining herself to touch only the tea and a couple of succulent fruits, she turned her back resolutely on the tray and rested her arms on the parapet, taking in the view of the city.

Her former accommodation was a pink speck far below. Along the winding road above it she saw a group of the sheikh's guards hiking uphill, evidently on a training exercise. After her journey to Al-Qasr, she knew the road was steep, but they scaled it effortlessly. The sheikh's opponents must be mad, thinking they could defeat such a disciplined force.

Yet they had killed Markaz's father and older brother, came the unwelcome thought. According to her reading, the old sheikh and his son had been flying home from a state visit when their plane had been destroyed by a rebel bomb.

If he'd stayed in Nazaar, her father could have been on board. As the editor of the *Nazaari Times*, he'd often traveled with the old sheikh to report on royal activities. He hadn't fared much better with a hit-and-run driver in Australia, but at least he'd had the better part of thirty years of living first.

Shaking off the sad thoughts, Simone returned to the bedroom, her spirits reviving as she put on the lovely clothes. With her makeup complete and the chiffon wrap improvised into a *hejab,* the scarf used by Nazaari women to cover their hair, she was ready when the sheikh's emissary came for her.

Fayed salaamed, looking approvingly at her appearance. "The sheikh is waiting for you, Miss Simone."

"Just Simone, please."

"Perhaps in Australia, but not here," he rumbled.

"But you call the sheikh Markaz. I heard you."

The giant frowned. "We grew up together and are brothers in all but name."

And with men it was different anyway. How on earth did men like Fayed cope with the reforms Markaz was gradually introducing? Did the rebels resist so fiercely to avoid losing their power over their womenfolk? Suddenly the modest clothing she'd put on so eagerly seemed more limiting than charming.

In a rush of defiance, she pulled off her *hejab* and let it float onto the bed, then fluffed out her hair, earning a curious look from Fayed. But he made no comment when she said, "I'm ready. Wouldn't want to keep the sheikh waiting."

Chapter 4

Waiting wasn't something Markaz tolerated well. Accustomed to having his needs met at the snap of his fingers, he had little use for patience. But this evening he was actually enjoying waiting for Simone, anticipation building like a fire inside him.

Deliberately he'd avoided reading the file his chief of security had placed on his desk an hour before. Hamal had assured him that she wasn't a threat to the royal family or the nation, so Markaz preferred to learn about Simone by delicious degrees as she chose to reveal herself to him.

Aware of her as a woman from the moment their eyes met, he was curious to see where the attraction led. The potency of the feeling surprised him. Not since his divorce from Natalie had he been so conflicted by a woman, drawn to her and knowing she wasn't for him. When he married again, and it was *when* because the kingdom required an heir, the woman would be of his own kind, as wedded to Nazaar as to him. This could be no more than an enjoyable interlude, but ending here.

Dissatisfaction at the thought made him get up and pace, halting as Fayed escorted her in. His friend salaamed and backed out, but not before Markaz had caught the indulgent look on Fayed's face. What was that supposed to mean? It wasn't as if he brought women to Markaz all the time. Not even most of the time. Had he sensed the undercurrent playing between Markaz and Simone? Maybe he should find Fayed a new assignment, where he couldn't read his boss's mind.

Just as well, Fayed wasn't doing it now. Markaz didn't know who'd been inspired to dress her in galabia and *sirwall,* but she wore them to the manner born. Her movements, graceful in Western dress, were even more fluid as she approached him, the tiny gold coins sewn into the costume's wrists and ankles tinkling like music. Talk about a recipe for seduction. He had a hard time keeping his mouth from dropping open.

Then he saw her looking around them. He'd deliberately ordered dinner served in the New York suite, named because the huge oak and sandblasted glass dining table, and leather-upholstered chairs all came from New York, along with the black waveform chaise, leather sofas and glass coffee tables that Markaz dodged as he paced around the living portion of the room.

The suite, actually two rooms linked by a wide archway, was larger than some New York apartments. In keeping with the American theme, the high ceilings were painted white and the walls covered in hand-painted, silk wallpaper in a subtle dragonfly design made of pearlized white sand. In place of the traditional Persian rugs, Aubusson carpets covered the marble floors. A wall mural of the Manhattan skyline by night created the impression of a view. The *New York Times* was flown in every day and placed in the suite.

After attending a United Nations conference, his father and mother had gone for a walk together. Seeing her looking nostalgically at the furniture displayed in the windows of the Domus Design Collection on Madison Avenue, he had ordered the entire ensemble delivered to Nazaar to surprise her. He'd purchased every item in the display down to the lighting, tableware and accessories, and had them shipped to Raisa.

Markaž's open-necked white shirt and black pants were Brooks Brothers, also chosen to suit the surroundings. So why did Simone look so angry? "Were you hoping for a more traditional setting? I can arrange it."

"Don't you think you've arranged enough for one evening, Your Highness?" she asked. "Does it amuse you to see me in fancy dress while you wear ordinary clothes?"

Despite using his title, she sounded anything but deferential. He drew himself up. "How does your choice of dress involve me?"

"My choice? Didn't you send these things to my room for me to wear tonight?"

He controlled his anger, just. "In my country, we value the presumption of innocence. Is it not the same in Australia?"

"Yes, but—"

"Hear me out. I chose this setting to make you feel at home, but I had no part in choosing your attire." Not that he had a problem with it, either, but he kept this to himself. She was angry enough, thinking he had amused himself at her expense. "Perhaps Amal selected the clothes, hoping to please you."

Some of the wind went out of her sails. "I'll certainly ask her. My apologies if I've misjudged you, Your Highness. But I should change before we dine."

Grudging her absence for even that length of time, he smiled to soften his objection. "I'd prefer you to stay as you are."

"I feel out of place, as if I belong in a different century."

As if she'd just walked out of the desert, one of the original inhabitants of his kingdom from many centuries before, he thought. Out loud he said, "You look breathtaking."

The compliment made her shift restively. "This clothing *is* comfortable."

"And undeniably becoming. Throughout our history, golden-haired beauties were treated as goddesses. Men went to war over them. Seeing you like this, it isn't hard to understand why."

He had the satisfaction of watching color rush into her cheeks. Not as tough as she pretended then. His anticipation notched higher.

Were there any more ways she could look idiotic in front of the sheikh, Simone asked herself. Not only did she look and feel out of place alongside his tailored—and modern—elegance, she'd accused the country's ruler of setting her up.

The more she thought about it, the more likely it seemed that he was right, and Amal had intended the clothes as a treat. The woman couldn't have known that the sheikh planned a Western-style evening for his guest. Thank goodness she'd discarded the *hejab* at the last minute.

She had to admit the flowing galabia and pants made

her feel delicate and feminine, although she would have preferred to see Markaz also in traditional dress. Because this way pointed up differences between them she'd rather overlook? Surely she wasn't that foolish?

Seating herself on the sofa Markaz indicated, she felt the leather shape itself to her body while the galabia drifted in graceful folds around her. She might feel like a fish out of water, but everything in the suite was in excellent taste. What was the story behind it?

The sheikh dropped into an armchair at right angles to her, crossing an ankle over one knee. Reaching over he pressed a control concealed in the arm of the chair.

Seconds later a maid glided in with champagne and canapés on a gold tray, set it on the glass-topped table between them, bowed to the sheikh then left as silently as she'd come.

When he handed her a drink, Simone's fingers tightened around the stem of the glass. She was probably destroying his carefully orchestrated mood—or maybe wanted to—by asking, "Have you learned anything more about Natalie, Your Highness?"

He frowned into his drink. "I have given orders to be interrupted if there is any news. And tonight I am merely Markaz."

He could never be merely anything. Even in dark pants and a monogrammed white shirt superbly tailored to fit his broad physique, he looked every inch a monarch. The open-necked shirt hinted at a smooth, muscular chest, and the pants were taut over his legs and hips. Without the traditional headdress, his hair was thick and slightly springy, cut just above his collar and looking as if it would curl naturally when wet.

A lightning image of him in the shower, the water

streaming down his sleek olive flanks sent a jet of excitement arrowing through her. She gulped champagne to
quench the fire as much as her thirst. Not a sight she would
see in her lifetime.

She was woman enough to want. But realist enough to
recognize when a desire was bad for her. She'd ended one
relationship because the man became too controlling.
Markaz was control on a stick.

Putting him into a Western setting didn't help, as her
father had proved. Despite thirty years of living in Australia,
he'd never changed his belief that his word was law simply
because he was male. Much as he'd loved his daughter,
Simone knew she would have ranked second if her mother
had borne a son. Common sense told her Markaz's view
would be even more rigid, because of who he was.

Since when did common sense ever win out over
desire?

It was going to this time. She inclined her head.
"Markaz then. How does a royal palace in Nazaar come
to have such a Western-looking room?"

As he explained about Norah and his father, she regarded the decor with new eyes. "What an extravagant,
romantic gesture. Was your mother delighted?"

"Of course. She still spends time here when she feels
homesick."

"Or when she wants to feel close to your father,"
Simone said.

Pain flashed across his face, instantly masked. "Indeed.
My family and the country are all poorer for his loss."

And Markaz himself? He'd been in America when his
father and brother were killed ten years before, never expecting to inherit the throne. She'd brushed up on Nazaar's
history on the Internet before leaving Australia. Now she

wondered how Markaz had felt without father or older brother to guide him, knowing he could be the rebels' next target, yet continuing the reform process anyway.

He leaned back, the crystal flute held between two long fingers. "Tell me how you come to wear our clothing so well."

"I'm flattered you think I do."

He nodded. "It's more fact than compliment. Right now you look more Nazaari than Australian."

"Perhaps because of my blood," she murmured.

Ah, now they were coming to it. The reason she looked so at home in the kingdom. "You have Nazaari ancestry?"

She took a sip of champagne. "My parents are from Nazaar. They moved to Australia before I was born."

Glad that he'd resisted the temptation to read her file, Markaz let a mouthful of champagne slide down his throat then put the glass down. She was more intoxicating than any drink, and he wanted to give her his full attention. "Your people are from the desert?"

"My mother's from Raisa. My father came from the desert. He died in a road accident a few months ago."

"My condolences."

The response sounded sincere. Of course, he'd suffered his share of loss and knew how she felt. "Thank you. They had a good life in Australia."

"They never returned to their homeland?"

"By the time the borders were open, they had settled where they were. I think my father was afraid he'd find more change than he wanted to see."

Markaz's eyes turned cold. "They were against the reform process?"

"No." She gave the single word all the emphasis she could. "The very opposite. It was because my father supported the old sheikh that they were forced to leave. He was warned that he and my mother would be killed if he continued to write in favor of the reforms. He would have taken his chances, but he loved my mother too much to risk her." Simone took a deep breath. "His name was Ali al Hasa."

Markaz looked astonished. "You're the daughter of Ali al Hasa? I was only a child when he left, but I heard a great deal about him. My father considered him a friend."

Tears of pleasure misted her eyes and she brushed them away. But not before he'd seen them. "Don't be ashamed of your tears, Simone. They do both our fathers honor."

She'd known her father had had friends at the palace, but until now had never fully understood how respected he'd been. How hard he must have found it to leave everything behind and start all over again.

"Sheikh Kemal provided Ali with an introduction to other expatriates living in Australia," Markaz told her.

Until now she hadn't known that the old sheikh himself had opened doors for her father. "That probably helped him to start his newsletter in Australia. I worked on it with him for a time, until I went into business for myself."

"You must have a good command of our language."

It took a moment to realize that Markaz had spoken to her in Arabic. "I speak the language less ably than most people in Nazaar speak English," she answered in the same tongue. "I hope to improve my skills during my visit."

"Then you shall have the opportunity," he said, switching back to English. "I shall assign Amal as your teacher."

"Surely she has more than enough to do? She told me she's studying at university."

"She will do as I command."

"I don't want you to pressure her on my account. It isn't fair."

She saw him blink at her bluntness, but it passed without comment. "Fairness is important to you?"

"Of course. Isn't it why you're putting your life on the line to pursue reforms?"

He tilted his glass to her. "You are indeed your father's daughter."

She inclined her head in response. "I take that as a compliment."

"Then why do you not use the name, al Hasa?"

"Before I was born my father changed the family name to Hayes, to fit in or to protect us, I don't know. He saw no need to discuss his thoughts with a daughter."

Markaz's keen gaze sharpened. "You are troubled by the natural order of things?"

Unconsciously she straightened her back. "There's nothing natural about the superiority of one sex over another."

His shoulders lifted eloquently. "Not natural, perhaps. But inevitable. Someone has to take the lead."

"*Take* being the operative word," she stated.

With care he chose a canapé and bit into it. She'd annoyed him, she saw from the tense set of his shoulders and jaw. So what? He wasn't *her* sheikh and his traditions weren't hers, except through her genes.

He was still the monarch and her host, she reminded herself. "I'm sorry for speaking out of turn, Your Highness," she said in Arabic, fearing the words would stick in her throat in English.

His dismissive gesture might have been for her manner or her opinions. "No matter. As the reforms proceed, change is coming soon enough."

Did his people regret or embrace the changes? Probably a little of both, she decided. What man would willingly share his authority with another, male or female, unless he had no choice? Even Markaz himself might find reform more attractive in theory than in practice.

She hadn't missed his reaction when she came in, as if Fayed had served her up to the sheikh on a plate. That would have to stop if men and women became equal. The right of the ruler to dictate women's behavior would be washed away under the new social order.

Female clothing would need to change, too. In Nazaari culture, the outfit she wore was designed to be concealing and revealing by turns. The flowing fabric made even the most clumsy wearer appear graceful, with the coins at wrists and ankles sending a musical message of availability.

In fairness, low-slung jeans and a T-shirt could send the same message, she told herself. A lot had to do with the attitude of the person wearing them. Realizing that she'd been leaning toward Markaz in a pose he might misread as female fascination, she moved farther away and crossed her arms in the universal body language of disinterest.

She'd been read like a book, she saw when the corners of his mouth lifted. He knew he interested her. Maybe the Nazaari people had it right all these centuries, she thought, irritated with herself. Segregating the sexes and veiling the women from men's eyes made life a lot less complicated. "Is change so desirable then?" she asked.

"Would you rather accept limits to your freedom than deal with what is between us?" he answered her question with his own.

"Of course not." Too late, she saw the trap. "I mean, there's nothing…"

He moved so quickly that he was alongside her on the sofa before she could react. "We both know there is. The kind of connection between us is rare, and not to be denied."

"Perhaps in your culture, Your Highness."

"In any culture. I notice you use my title when you want to create a barrier between us."

Whatever worked, she thought, all too afraid that nothing would. He wasn't touching her or making any move to do so, but she *felt* his nearness in every fiber of her being. And wanted more, pity help her.

She wanted him to pull her into his arms and kiss her, taking the initiative for them both. The very idea made her mind spin and her blood race as she imagined how that would feel. The low sounds he would make as he claimed her mouth, and the urgent way she would press against him. The dizzying dance of tongue to tongue and skin to skin as he slid his hands over her throat and shoulders.

Only as her back started to arch did reality come crashing back. Arousal warred with anger for letting her mind run away with her. None of that was going to happen. Except that her body thrummed as fiercely as if it just had.

"I don't need barriers between us, Markaz," she said, the unsteadiness in her voice belying the words. "Because nothing will happen that I don't sanction."

He let his dark gaze linger on her mouth for unsettling seconds. "Of that, you may be in no doubt. Now let us eat."

Accepting his hand to help her up, she thought his promise had come too easily. He must be very sure she would eventually give in to him, she thought, not at all sure herself that he wasn't right.

The food was a welcome distraction and for once she was glad to give her full attention to the meal without the distraction of small talk. The Western menu wouldn't have been out of place in any five-star restaurant back home. The first course was a whole fish poached in wine and herbs, followed by Kobe beef with lobster and truffles then a zabaglione so light it dissolved in her mouth.

Only when coffee was served did he resume their conversation. By then she felt steadier. She'd had the sense to drink ice water with the meal, to stop her imagination running away with her again. If she pleaded tiredness and got out of here soon, the tactic might even work.

But Markaz had other ideas. He called for liqueurs to be served with the coffee. The pale gold liquid known as *Ayn Zakat*—"spring of charity"—had been her father's favorite drink, and her throat tightened at the memory.

Markaz watched her hold the glass to the light, admiring the fine particles of real gold suspended in the liquid. "Do you know the legend of *Ayn Zakat?*"

She nodded. "According to my father, the drink bubbled up out of a barren plain, sustaining the Nazaari people after Alexander the Great's army drove them from their homes into the desert in ancient times. No proof of the spring has ever been found."

"You don't believe such myths?"

"Let's say, I prefer a touch more reality."

"Will you follow your father's example and tell your children our legends?"

At present the odds were against the need arising, but she didn't say so. "Probably, but I'll also tell them it's only a story." Disturbingly, a picture popped into her mind of her sitting on the edge of a bed, telling bedtime tales to a smaller reflection of herself. The thought brought an unexpected jolt.

He picked up something of her thoughts. "You do not wish to be a mother?"

"For that, you need a father."

"Is there no man likely to fill the role?"

One, she thought and instantly quashed the thought. Women were hardwired to regard strong male specimens as potential husbands and fathers, regardless of suitability. And it was hard to picture a less suitable match for her than Markaz.

"None," she said firmly. Before he could pursue the question she changed the subject. "By most standards, ours is a small family. During my visit, I hope to locate one of my father's relatives. In Raisa when I made inquiries, I was told that he might be a member of your household guard."

"Al Hasa is a common enough name, but I can think of none in my employ."

Surely even the sheikh of sheikhs couldn't know every one of hundreds of staff by name, she thought. But thinking of the phone call to Australia earlier, Simone couldn't give up. If finding her mother's lost family member could give Sara the peace of mind she needed, Simone would find him.

"This liqueur is delicious," she said, changing the subject. "Although I am surprised…"

"That alcohol is openly enjoyed in Nazaar? My father abolished many prohibitions including that one. He passed laws ensuring moderation, but some rebels want us to return to total abstinence. Even though this very drink is said to be a gift from the Creator."

A crystal bowl shaped like a full-blown rose held a selection of handmade chocolates and he offered one to her. When she bit into it, an unexpected mix of chocolate and chili burst on her tongue. Unusual, but delicious. "Are there many rebels left?" she asked.

Selecting a chocolate, he took a moment to answer. "Many fewer than there used to be in your father's day. They have also splintered into smaller groups. Some make their point peacefully through the ballot box, and have been elected to the ruling council where they provide me with, shall we say, lively opposition."

Her spirits rose. If Markaz tolerated rebel candidates in his government, perhaps he wouldn't be angry if he found out Yusef had concealed his past. She realized she was staking a lot on locating her half uncle at the palace, but she had little else to go on for now.

"Of course, there are always the hotheads," he went on.

She shuddered. "Like the man pursuing me at Al-Qasr this morning."

"Yes. A few rebels still choose bloodshed over reason."

This made no sense. "Why, if they already have a voice in your government?"

He finished his drink and set the glass down with a crash. "This particular group doesn't want a voice. They want control. Our people see that moving with the times isn't the end of the world. Forcing them back into the old ways can only be done at the cost of lives, but a small group of rebels are prepared to kill to impose their will. They won't stop until they take over the government."

Simone thought of Natalie's warning. "Doesn't it worry you to be their prime target?"

"I sleep well enough at night." He sat forward. "The ruler who pleases everybody, achieves nothing."

She didn't know whether to be impressed by his courage or frustrated by his light tone. "An old Arab saying?"

"One I made up only a few seconds ago."

"You need a secretary on hand to record these pearls of wisdom."

"Most wisdom is only common sense in fancy words," he pointed out, then lowered his voice. "Besides, not everything said tonight should be for the record."

The ground shifted under her feet. He didn't elaborate, but his message was clear. He still wanted the evening to become personal. What did she want?

Since that soul-searing moment when their eyes met across the barrier at Al-Qasr—was it only hours ago?—she'd felt a connection between them. Like an invisible link, it pulsed with heat and energy. At will, he could reel her in along it like a fish on a line, she suspected. He wasn't doing it now, only watching her and waiting for her reaction. Should she remain aloof, or let herself be reeled in?

Before she could make up her mind, a tall, ascetic-looking man with a black beard bowed himself in and Markaz greeted him. "This is Hamal al Nawi, chief of royal security," Markaz informed her.

The man bowed to her. "Forgive the intrusion, madam. I have urgent news for His Highness."

Hamal looked from her to the sheikh, and she saw Markaz give a slight nod of his head. Indicating that Hamal could speak freely in front of her, or advising him against it? The two men began to converse softly in Arabic.

"For goodness' sake, tell me what you have to say, preferably in English," she burst out, too worried to risk any misunderstanding. Protocol be damned. She had not only seen Natalie abducted, the same man had come after Simone, forcing Markaz to offer her refuge. How much worse could the news get?

Chapter 5

A lot worse, she soon learned. Switching to English, Hamal told them that Natalie's body had been found in the desert. She had been poisoned and her body dumped some distance off the main highway. Her car had been found several miles farther along the road, wiped clean of any useful evidence. The police were checking it over thoroughly, but the man Simone thought of as Business Suit had vanished and there were no witnesses.

After Hamal bowed and left the room, the sheikh returned his attention to her. "There are no witnesses except you."

She didn't hesitate. "I can't let Natalie's death count for nothing. When we met she must have known she'd been poisoned, but all she wanted was to get a message to you."

The sheikh's breath gusted out and his voice was cold as he said, "Completing her mission was always the most important thing to her."

Simone felt her eyebrows lift. "Her mission?"

"She worked for her government as a specialist in Middle Eastern affairs."

"A spy?"

"She preferred the term *government agent,*" he said. "I didn't know it when we met, but she'd been recruited as a student. Getting to know me was her first assignment."

No wonder he sounded so cold, Simone thought. What he'd taken for mutual attraction had been based on expedience. "Was that why things didn't work out between you?"

"The truth about her work didn't emerge until much later. She had been assigned to befriend me and sound me out about an alliance between our countries. At the time, I wasn't expected to succeed to the throne, but her bosses were thinking ahead, with good reason as it turned out. Then she did the unthinkable and fell in love. Marrying me was her idea, not her boss's."

Did he truly believe that? Simone wondered. "She must have cared a great deal to try and get a message to you, knowing she hadn't long to live."

"It would be like her to fight to her last breath to do what she believed was right. She loved what she did and being at the center of power. I suspect my attraction had as much to do with my position, as with love. When I became ruler and we left America to live in Nazaar, she couldn't continue working for her government. She hated the restrictions on her life here and missed her work so much that she asked me to end our marriage. Our parting was less than amicable."

"Her message must have been serious to bring her back here," Simone suggested. "Why didn't she just call you?"

His mouth hardened into a grim line. "She had identified a traitor within the palace, and feared her message being intercepted."

Simone drank the last of her liqueur like medicine. "If only she'd had more time, you'd know the traitor's name."

"She didn't offer any clues? Anywhere for my people to start?"

"Only the ring. I'm sorry."

"You did all you could. More than I have a right to expect."

Because unlike Natalie, Simone had no personal involvement. Her only reason for passing on the incomplete message was because she also believed in doing what was right. She hoped it wasn't going to get one or both of them killed. "What will you do now?"

"Report Natalie's death and the failure of her mission to her people. As soon as our police complete their investigation, her remains will be returned to her family in America. In the meantime, I shall carry on my duties."

"You won't take any steps to protect yourself?"

"The rebel faction that killed her has wanted to be rid of my line for a long time. Without knowing the traitor's identity, I'd be hiding from shadows. Drawing out my enemies might put an end to this futile struggle."

"It might also put an end to your life."

He seared her with a look. "Don't start caring about me, Simone. That was Natalie's mistake, and ultimately she paid for it with her life."

Vehemently Simone shook her head. "Natalie's work was her undoing. If she'd stayed here, this wouldn't have happened. From what you've told me, if she believed she was right, she'd have gone ahead regardless of the risk."

"You and she have a lot in common. Both women of high principles and moral certainty."

Thinking of what she hadn't told him about Yusef, Simone felt chilled. She was also guilty of deceiving him. "You can't say that about me, you hardly know me."

"I know enough to want you out of here tomorrow. Fayed will take you to your room and post a guard through the night. Tomorrow you will be on the first plane back to Australia."

"This isn't about getting me to safety, is it?" she demanded as light dawned. "It's about getting me away from you, because you believe you're the real target."

"We're playing with words. You're leaving tomorrow."

She jumped to her feet. "Your ex-wife died because she wanted to help you. You can't betray her by abandoning democratic principles whenever they don't serve your will."

His expression took on a dangerous hardness. "Are you telling me how to run my country?"

Refusing to flinch, she stood, meeting his gaze as evenly as she could. "I'm telling you what you need to hear, Your Highness. I'm not stupid. I don't want to die. But I'm the only one who knows Natalie's killer on sight. Until he and his cohorts are stopped, I'm not safe anywhere. At least here, I have Fayed and your guards as protection."

"And one of them could be a murderous traitor," he ground out. "But you're right about Natalie's killer. Very well, you may remain here under royal protection until he is identified, then you will leave. In the meantime, you will not challenge my authority again. Understood?"

"Perfectly, Your Highness." Understanding and complying were two different things.

He began to tick points off on his fingers. "Your best protection will be to conceal yourself among the women of my household. From this moment you will dress and act as they do. Amal will be your tutor."

She opened her mouth to remind him that Amal had

more than enough to do already, then remembered her promise not to challenge him.

"Whenever you leave the palace, you will be veiled. Your blond hair stands out like a beacon."

"That makes sense."

"You will speak only Arabic in public." His mouth tilted. "You wanted to practice your language skills. Consider this your opportunity."

"Agreed? Anything else?"

"Yes. You will kiss me."

Stopped in her tracks, she couldn't think of a thing to say in any language except "What?"

"You heard me. I have been curious to taste your mouth all evening. You have willingly placed yourself under my authority. Now learn what that means."

Hearing that he had thought of kissing her, even as she'd imagined herself in his arms shocked her. Oh, she'd known the attraction was far from one-sided, but had never expected such a blatant admission. Or a command to fulfill his fantasy.

"Now listen, Your Highness…Markaz, I know we said no challenges, but that doesn't mean…didn't include…I'm not part of the package."

Unbending steel met her resistance. "You *are* the package, the one person Natalie's killer wants."

Evidently he wasn't the only one. "I don't see what that has to do with being commanded to kiss you."

His expression turned wintry. "You don't see, and there's the problem. With my experience of the rebels' ways, I could become aware of a danger that you fail to see, but by the time you've decided whether or not to do as I command, you're likely to be dead."

Rocked to her core, she stared at him, not willing to admit to feeling betrayed. "The order to kiss you was a *test?*"

He spread his hands wide. "One you failed. *Ma'alish,* it does not matter. You will go home tomorrow. My government has friends among the Australian authorities. Through them I will arrange for your protection once you are back on your own soil."

Her father had often said her need to question his every edict would one day get her into trouble. Now it seemed he was right. And perhaps Markaz was also right to send her packing before she got herself in any deeper. But it was unclear whether she was afraid of Natalie's killer or her feelings for the sheikh. Both reasons were valid. So why did the idea of leaving stick in her throat so?

Before she had the thought fully formed, she had stepped close to Markaz and linked her arms around his neck. She only had to tilt her head back a little to meet his startled gaze. Then before he could react, she fastened her mouth over his.

Fairly sure that no one had ever kissed the sheikh of sheikhs so impetuously, she had expected him to untangle himself from her arms and thrust her away. If he had done, she would have returned to her room and started packing.

Instead his arms clamped around her and she was pulled closer, swamped by the heat and strength pouring into her from him. She may as well have lit a fuse.

His exotic scent enveloped her like a cloud of pure desire. On his lips was the bittersweet *Ayn Zakat* they'd drunk, the taste more heady than before, spinning her senses into a vortex. He was leaner, harder than she'd thought possible, rocklike as he braced her. Under his protection, the only thing any woman would have to fear was him.

Yet fear was the last thing she felt. Excitement, yes. A rapt kind of passion that was so new and powerful, addiction seemed inevitable.

With his arms locked around her, his response was all too apparent through the folds of his clothing. This, too, made her feel exhilarated, giddy with her power to affect him. She parted her lips, inviting him to take more, still more.

Her knees gave as he pressed her back until she lay across the sofa with his body angled over hers. "Open your eyes," he growled.

She hadn't been aware of closing them, losing herself in sensation. Now she let her eyes flutter open, her breath snagging at the sight of his carved features as he lowered his head to her throat. A low moan emerged as his teeth grazed the sensitive skin there.

Kneeling above Simone, Markaz felt wild with desire. How long had it been since he'd wanted a woman so much? Needed them, yes. Satisfied himself as a man must do. But without this urgency to know and possess.

Ordering her to kiss him had been a test, but of himself as much as her. If she'd obeyed, he would have sent her away anyway, knowing he couldn't trust himself to keep her safe—at least not from him.

This was what he had feared. This was what he had wanted.

Now she was in his arms of her own accord, her lips as eager and giving as he'd imagined since his first sight of her at Al-Qasr. Was it only this morning? He felt as if he'd waited a lifetime for her. For this.

The muted cries in her throat and her bowed body told him he was giving as much pleasure as he was taking. And by his oath, there was pleasure here. Pleasure and the promise of ecstasy. His body quaked with anticipation. The blood throbbed through him, pooling in his loins, making him ready to explode.

Dragging the neckline of her galabia down, he heard the delicate fabric give but paid it no heed, wanting only to glory in her revealed beauty. Later he would clothe her in the finest garments in the kingdom, cloth of gold and silver, the most precious jewels. For now he needed to see, to taste, to touch all she was.

Overwhelmed by sensation, Simone wanted the experience to go on and on. Wanted Markaz to take her, as she would take him. Here in this room, its very existence the embodiment of one man's love for a woman. On this sofa cradling her as luxuriously as any bed.

Braced with one knee between hers, Markaz leaned over her, his mouth hot and hungry as it skimmed over the tops of her breasts. She moved restively, frustrated by the amount of clothing coming between them. Wanting it gone. Placing her hands on his broad chest, she pushed him away intending to shrug off the voluminous garment.

And stopped.

Seeing him above her, really seeing him, and realizing what she was contemplating sent a shock wave through her. "No," she insisted. "No, we have to stop."

Like a man surfacing from a dream, he levered himself away and dragged his fingers through his hair. His voice sounded smoky as he said, "It's what you invited. What we both want."

What she still wanted, she thought in the part of her mind refusing to listen to reason. Hearing the confusion in his voice and seeing in his face the wild desire she'd ignited, she wondered if she was mad to stop him. They were both free agents. Both adults. Where was the harm?

Honesty forced her to say, "I know, but it's too soon. For me, anyway."

His mouth thinned. "You'd insult me by suggesting I make a habit of this?"

"I've no doubt that the reputation of Nazaari men as great lovers is deserved." After this how could she doubt? And the experience had barely begun. "Growing up, I had enough of my father ruling my life because he felt his gender gave him the right. Other men have tried since, and I've left them high and dry."

"Now you'd do the same to me without benefit of trial."

Thinking of what form the trial had so nearly taken, she swallowed hard. "You spelled out your rules for letting me stay in Nazaar. You even ordered me to kiss you."

"For your own good."

She rolled her eyes. "My father's standard justification for his rules."

He placed his hands behind his neck and stretched his head against them. His whole body throbbed with unanswered needs. He wanted to be angry with her, but he couldn't. Her father had fled a Nazaar that was still feudal in many ways. Recreating the only life he'd known, Ali al Hasa wouldn't have been aware that his old lifestyle no longer existed except in his mind. Markaz knew of many children of migrants who were amazed to return and find that their parents were the ones frozen in time while their homeland had moved on.

Not used to justifying himself to anyone, he was surprised at his thinking. Even more by how much he wanted Simone. Forbidden fruit, al Nazaari? he asked himself, but knew the challenge went deeper. He wanted to understand her as much as he yearned to make love to her. "Then let me ask you to please disguise yourself as a member of my household until the murderer is caught." His tone emphasized that, this time, it was a request.

He had the satisfaction of seeing her lovely eyes widen and she said, "I thought you'd never ask."

Amal muttered disapprovingly as she mixed a verbena-scented potion in a bowl. "Are you sure this is what you want?"

"Markaz says my blond hair stands out like a beacon."

"All the same, we could cover it with a *hejab* if you have to go out. Or even a burka that would leave only your eyes exposed. Changing your beautiful hair color seems like a sin."

Stretched out full length on a chaise longue with her head tilted back over a basin, Simone couldn't imagine herself swathed from head to toe in black, looking at the world through a fabric grille over her eyes. These days only very elderly Nazaari women wore the full burka. Younger women preferred to frame their hair with the *hejab* scarf or leave their hair uncovered.

"Like most natural blondes, I've often wondered what I'd look like as a brunette. Do your worst."

Spreading the thick lather over Simone's hair, Amal made a clucking sound of concern. "My worst may ruin your hair altogether. Have you thought of that?"

They'd already gone over this when the sheikh took Amal into his confidence earlier that morning. "We can't call in a professional. Markaz had my name added to a tour group flying out this morning. My continued presence has to be a secret known to as few people as possible. By the time you're finished, I'll look like any one of His Highness's conquests."

Working the mixture through Simone's locks, Amal smiled. "I have lived at the palace on and off since Markaz's marriage ended. No woman has claimed his attention for long."

"So he's fickle?"

Above her, Amal's slight shoulders lifted. "He is a man with a man's needs. But he does not let his heart rule his head."

Good advice for her, too, Simone thought. She closed her eyes and let herself drift as Amal worked the color through her hair. The massaging sensation was hypnotic. She was glad Markaz had told Amal the truth, giving Simone someone she could confide in. The sheikh might think she was brave, but the reality of what she had committed herself to was starting to rattle her. What if someone within the palace was out to harm Markaz? Wouldn't she also be in their sights? Amal could even be the traitor. Immediately Simone dismissed the thought. Apart from being his cousin, Amal's devotion to the sheikh was obvious.

While they waited for the color to take, Amal pulled up a seat opposite Simone. "It was late when Fayed brought you back to the women's quarters last night. Do you find my cousin attractive?"

"Who wouldn't?" Not that anything would come of it. *Should* come of it. "He's a very compelling man."

"He finds you compelling also."

His kiss had told her so, but she kept that to herself. "How do you know?"

"I know Markaz. He's shown no serious interest in a woman for many years. Until you."

"Only because I did him a favor and now need his protection."

Amal got up and checked the dye. "You may think so,

but I see him looking at you as if he can hardly believe you're real."

Simone shifted uncomfortably. "So quickly? That's impossible."

"I'm not saying he's in love yet," Amal denied. "Only that you've had a greater effect on him than you realize."

Or wanted to have. The *yet* also troubled Simone. She diverted Amal by asking about her daily life, equipping herself to deal with the new environment. "I gather it helps to like shopping," she said dryly.

"It's a favorite pastime of our women. You don't enjoy it?" Amal sounded disbelieving.

"Mainly I shop over the Internet."

"How can you see and touch the items on offer? Or share coffee with the shopkeepers?"

Uncivilized was the word she didn't use, but Simone heard it anyway. "I manage. However, I will shop for some of your heirloom embroidery for my business."

Amal brightened. "We'll go together as soon as Markaz declares it's safe."

Declaring the wait over, she sluiced tepid water through Simone's hair. The blow-drying stage followed, then she was handed a mirror. Holding the glass, Simone stifled a cry. Her hair gleamed red-gold like the sky at sunset, making her skin glow. "I look like pictures of my mother as a young woman. I used to wish I looked more like her."

"Now you do." Amal clapped her hands. "We'll complete the look with traditional clothing."

Simone set the mirror aside. "You'd risk lending me another galabia after I tore the first one?"

Amal looked puzzled. "What do you mean, another?"

"Didn't you set out traditional clothes for me to wear last night?"

"I heard Markaz order dinner served in the New York suite, so I knew your own Western clothes would be more appropriate. Unless…" She tapped a fingernail. "I saw Markaz's mother, Princess Norah, take some clothes into your room. But she would have known what Markaz planned. Why would she want you to dress unsuitably?"

Simone could work it out, or thought she could. Amal might not have been the only one to notice Markaz's interest in Simone. Sabotaging her appearance was one way to nip it in the bud. Simone would have to watch herself around the princess.

With Amal she had no such qualms. The young royal's enthusiasm was catching as she piled garments into Simone's arms. "Try this, and this. One of these. And this of course." She added jewelry to the armload.

Simone laughed. "Surely you don't mean I should wear them all at once?"

Amal took the garments from her and piled them in a divan. "Look, I'll show you. The galabia goes on first."

Divesting Simone of the cotton robe she'd worn for the hair treatment, Amal slid a straight-cut dress over Simone's upraised arms. The lovely silk was embroidered at wrists and chest, and fell in graceful folds to her feet.

Then she slid another, lighter layer over the galabia. This layer was also brightly embroidered in gold thread and was called a *thobe,* Amal explained. "Different styles are worn for different occasions."

Simone was familiar with the *sirwall,* the flowing, trouserlike garment worn under the dress and caught at the ankles with still more embroidery. She looked forward to studying the designs more closely, making some sketches and learning about their history from Amal.

"More layers?" she said as the young royal arranged a fine, silky cloak around her shoulders.

"This is the abaya," she explained. Finally she wound a length of fabric around Simone's head. "The headpiece ensures privacy, especially if you veil like this." She fixed a gauzy cloth over the lower half of Simone's face.

Expecting to feel stifled, Simone was surprised to find she felt mysterious and exotic. Dressing this way all the time might have less appeal, but as an experience it was excitingly different. Coupled with her new dark hair, all trace of her normal appearance had been erased.

Amal took her hand and threaded each finger with a ring, the rings in turn attached to a chunky bracelet. "This is a traditional piece of Nazaari jewelry, popular with young women during celebrations. Most royal women wear a fortune in jewelry."

Simone lowered her hand and her eyes. "As you wish, Princess Amal."

Delighted laughter greeted her meek pose. "Now you are a true Nazaari lady."

"I'm not sure how long I can keep up the subservient routine," Simone said with a laugh.

"May I tell you a secret? It's an act to beguile our men into thinking we're demure and biddable. After marriage, they find out the awful truth, that we have minds and spirits of our own, but by then it's too late."

Perfect courtship camouflage, as well as a disguise to protect her from Natalie's killer, Simone reflected. The thought sobered her. This wasn't a game of dress-up, but a life-and-death necessity. She arranged the abaya around her shoulders as Amal had demonstrated. "Thank you for doing this for me."

Amal caught her mood. "I wish it was for a different reason. I don't like to think of you in danger."

"Or Markaz. He's the real target."

"He is strong. And well guarded."

As long as it wasn't by a traitor, Simone hoped.

A commotion at the entrance to the women's quarters sent fear jolting through her and she pulled the abaya up to cover her head. But one of the teenage royals, a girl of no more than sixteen, ran up to them. "Amal, you have to help me. Something terrible has happened."

Chapter 6

With a worried look at Simone, Amal grasped the young woman by the shoulders. "Calm down, Bibi. Tell me what's wrong."

Bibi gulped hard. "Some police officers came to meet with Sheikh Markaz. Abdl saw them arrive and panicked. They caught him when he tried to sneak out of my room."

"Oh no. You gave the sheikh your word you wouldn't see Abdl alone again until you finished school."

"I know, but I love him." The girl's reedy voice rose to a wail. "They took him away in the police vehicle. What am I going to do?"

Amal exchanged concerned looks with Simone. "You should have thought of that before breaking your promise. You know how much Sheikh Markaz hates lies and deception."

Too distressed to pay attention to Simone, Bibi hadn't

given her a second glance. Now Simone felt uneasy, thinking of her own small deception in not mentioning Yusef's past to the sheikh. If he was this tough on a young girl in love, how would he react to Simone's evasion? The thought was unsettling.

No doubt the police had come to see Markaz to discuss the investigation into Natalie's murder. Simone had given them her own statement earlier in the day. At the sheikh's request, she'd been interviewed at the palace, and the police had agreed to keep her where-abouts quiet.

"Why was Abdl taken away?" she asked in Arabic.

Amal answered. "It sounds like something Markaz would have set up for show, to teach Bibi a lesson. Markaz knows Abdl isn't a rebel. His family is among the sheikh's closest friends. He'll probably be released into their custody later with orders not to show his face at the palace except in his parents' company for a few more years."

"Years?" Bibi wailed again. "I can't bear it."

"Yes, you can. If you're a good student, Sheikh Markaz may let Abdl visit you, although not in your room."

The teenager had calmed down visibly. "Will you speak to him for me?"

"I'll see what I can do."

Bibi threw her arms around Amal. "Thank you, thank you."

"Thank me by studying hard."

"I will." Finally she threw a curious glance at Simone. "And thank you…"

"This is my cousin, Sima," Amal supplied before Simone could answer.

"Thank you, Sima."

Her parents had sometimes called her that as a pet

name. Hearing it now gave her an odd feeling of belonging. "You're welcome, Bibi."

When the teenager had gone, Simone pulled off the abaya and sank onto the chaise longue. "Shades of Romeo and Juliet."

"Except that their families aren't in conflict. They are simply too young for anything more than friendship yet."

"Do many girls like Bibi live at the palace?"

"The royal family is large and scattered. Some branches are from desert communities where there are limited educational facilities. Our society frowns on the young princesses living alone, so the palace is the most suitable environment for them while they complete school or university."

"Bibi paid me no more attention than she would the wallpaper. She completely accepted me as your cousin, Sima. Quick thinking on the name, too."

"It's the nearest Nazaari name to your own, so you'll remember to answer to it if addressed. No one will give Cousin Sima a second look."

Knowing her life could depend on it, Simone nodded. "Then I'd better make sure it stays that way."

Simone found out the next day that one person she didn't have to fool with her disguise was Markaz's mother, Princess Norah. She hadn't expected to have much to do with the princess, but was summoned to join her for lunch in her apartments.

Lunch was the main meal of the day in Nazaar—a time when families gathered at home late in the afternoon, depending on their schedules. But Norah preferred to eat alone in her own quarters.

She felt a moment of panic when a maid came to fetch

"Sima" from the women's quarters and escort her through the palace to the wing Norah occupied. The older woman plainly didn't like her. Why would she send for her?

She soon found out. "My son told me what you did for him, and requested that I make you feel at home," she said when Simone was seated across from her on a cushioned divan pulled up to a low table. The abaya lay on the seat beside her. With her newly colored hair, she felt safe enough with her face uncovered among the women, at least within the palace.

A maid served them cardamom-flavored coffee in tiny cups then left them alone. A tall, gaunt woman whose tragic losses were etched on her sharp features, Norah looked anything but welcoming. Simone was distracted by the feeling that she'd seen Norah before, although they'd never met as far as Simone knew.

"That's kind of you," Simone said.

"Not at all. Markaz is the sheikh."

Her meaning was clear. Her son's word was law and Norah would obey him, no matter how distasteful she found the request. "Nevertheless, I appreciate the courtesy," Simone murmured.

"The hair and clothes are an improvement," Norah said as if thinking out loud. "As long as you don't plan on remaining here after Natalie's killer is caught."

Simone sipped the strong, bitter coffee, mentally counting to ten. Letting her temper betray her would get them nowhere. "I can identify the man who dragged her into the car. But he also saw me."

A flicker of something—sympathy?—flashed across Norah's expression, then was gone. "Had Natalie chosen a different path, she might still be alive."

Lowering the cup, Simone said, "This must be hard for

you, too. Dealing with so much loss, and worrying about your son's safety, as well."

Norah fixed her with a gimlet look. "Don't think you can manipulate me as easily as you did my son. When you arrived I saw how he looked at you, as if you were a new toy for his pleasure. I may be Nazaari now, but I know how Western women think, and the strategies they use to wrap men around their little fingers."

It was on the tip of her tongue to ask the older woman if she spoke from experience. After all, she'd managed to marry her own sheikh. But again Simone held her tongue. Her father would have been proud of her. "With respect, Princess Norah, I'm not Natalie."

"No, but you are her clone. When she decided to return to her old life in America, she hurt Markaz. I won't let it happen again."

"So the first night I was here, you provided me with the wrong clothes, hoping I'd look foolish when I dined with Markaz in the New York suite."

Norah was trembling with anger now. "My husband created that room for me. Markaz had no right to entertain a woman there."

The way she spat out *woman, floozy* would have done, as well. "That wasn't my fault," Simone observed. "As you said, he is the sheikh of sheikhs."

It was the right thing to say, she noticed as Norah visibly subsided. But Simone felt shaken. The murder of a husband and son, and now a former daughter-in-law, was enough to unbalance anybody.

But Norah sounded calm enough when she ordered her maid to serve lunch, then slipped into the role of hostess as if the previous conversation hadn't happened.

Many of the dishes placed in front of Simone were

familiar from her parents' home, but she didn't interrupt when Norah explained them to her. "This is called *youlanji*, a meatless dish of stuffed vegetables. And the lentils and rice topped with brown onions is *mujadarra*."

There was roast chicken flavored with lemon juice, a spinachlike leafy green cooked in broth and served over rice, a variety of salads and the bread Simone's mother used to bake at home, called *khubz*. The aromas alone were enough to make her homesick.

She'd telephoned her mother again after breakfast. This time they were able to talk, but hearing that Simone had no news of Yusef, Sara had become tearful. How was she going to cope if Simone wasn't able to find out anything more?

Too tense to do more than pick at the array of dishes, Simone wondered what she was doing here. If it was only to warn her off Markaz, little did Norah know there was no need. However scorching the kiss they'd exchanged, Simone had no intention of getting involved with him. She knew his type only too well. If she needed additional evidence. Norah's deference to her son's dictates was more effective than anything she might have said.

Simone hadn't seen him since their shared dinner two nights ago, so he wasn't pining for her company, either. Fayed had arranged the police interview, and Amal had done everything else. Busy with his affairs of state, Markaz probably hadn't given her a second thought.

By the time a platter of fresh fruit was brought, Simone had bitten her tongue so often she was surprised it was still attached. Out of politeness she picked at some grapes and figs, complimenting her hostess on the quality and variety of local and imported fruits, as she knew was expected of her. But when she started to rise, Norah stayed her with a gesture.

"Markaz tells me you are interested in Nazaari embroidery."

Where was this leading? "I run a business on the Internet selling heirloom designs and supplies internationally."

Norah nodded. "So I'm told. The palace has the largest collection of traditional embroidery in the country. Markaz thinks you should see some of the royal collection."

Although excited at the prospect, Simone reined in her enthusiasm, reluctant to extend the uncomfortable encounter. Helping Markaz might have earned his mother's gratitude, but not her friendship. Norah's experience with Natalie had seen to that. So Simone said, "Thank you, but the thought is enough. I don't want to take up your time."

Norah's bitterness surfaced again. "I have little else to take it up. We shall carry out my son's wishes and inspect the collection."

Somewhat less gracefully, Simone followed, arranging her abaya so it shadowed her face. This was her first chance to explore outside the women's quarters in daylight, so she looked around with interest. Every arched window offered a view over the city of Raisa or the surrounding hills and valleys. Vaulted zigzag passages connected the different sections, with rooms opening off them. Engravings, woven hangings, weapons and murals decorated the walls. In the manner of a tour guide, Norah pointed out the apartments serving as offices and reception rooms for Markaz, his government ministers and the members of his court.

As Norah swept up to a large, richly decorated set of doors, a guard rushed to open them, and Simone followed her into a huge reception room taking up two levels. The lower area had a fine mosaic floor and walls covered with marble and inscriptions. One she managed to translate as "An hour of justice is worth a thousand months of prayer."

This must be where Markaz held court, she thought, remembering her parents telling her that the sheikh was the first and last resort in matters of law. There were Western-style courts, too, and a conventional justice system. But by ancient tradition, the sheikh dispensed justice wherever he might be.

A large raised area set into a great bay window opposite the main doors added weight to her theory. Markaz would sit there to hear petitions from his people, apart from them, but not too far above them, in keeping with custom.

Norah led the way to a domed chamber off the main hall. "Much of the royal collection is stored in climate-controlled vaults. These exhibits are rotated on a regular basis to protect the delicate materials," she explained as she handed Simone a glossy catalog printed in Arabic and English.

Stumbling into Aladdin's cave wouldn't have left Simone more spellbound. In front of her were examples of piecework she'd only read about and never thought to actually see. She could hardly believe her good fortune when Norah unlocked the nearest case and raised the glass cover. "I trust you know better than to handle the exhibits."

"I wouldn't dream of it." She was more than content to feast her eyes on the intricate needlework. Hard to believe how such tiny stitching had been done without a magnifying glass.

Only her respect for the fragility of the work kept Simone's hands firmly at her sides as she leaned closer to inspect every detail. Some of the motifs were new to her. Were they still in use? The copyrights available?

Belatedly she realized she was ignoring her hostess, and straightened. "I'm sorry, I'm getting carried away."

Norah turned from gazing out a window. "Take all the time you like. It's rare to find a visitor who fully appreciates our decorative arts."

She sounded almost human. "Are you interested in embroidery, Princess?"

"Only as it relates to Oriental history in general. I'm writing a book about Süleyman the Magnificent, the great leader of the Ottoman Empire."

Simone nodded. Reigning in the early-to-mid-fifteen hundreds, he was not only a powerful military leader, but also a poet who encouraged his empire's art and culture to flourish. "What inspired you to tackle such a substantial project?"

"Present-day Nazaari culture owes a lot to his influence."

"Judging by the quality of this exhibition, you won't lack for research materials." And they would be only the tip of the iceberg, Simone thought on a flash of envy.

Norah suddenly seemed to realize she was thawing out, and drew her shoulders back. "Indeed. The palace has a magnificent library dating back to the thirteenth century. I can show you if you wish."

"I've taken up more than enough of your time for now. I'm happy to return to the women's quarters and study the catalog."

Norah didn't bother to mask her relief. "I'll have someone show you the way."

Simone could have found her own way, but sensed that Norah wouldn't consider her duty done until her guest was safely back where she belonged. The thought frustrated her. How on earth was she to find out if her father's half brother was among the palace guards if all her time was spent in the women's quarters?

"Would you mind if I walk in the gardens before returning to my room?" she asked.

If she'd suggested taking off all her clothes in the middle of the reception hall, Norah wouldn't have looked more taken aback. "Alone?"

"I don't want to delay you, Princess. As an only child, I'm used to being by myself."

"After what happened at Al-Qasr, it's too risky."

She sounded as if she cared. "There are guards every dozen feet. I'll stay within the inner courtyard where they can see me." And more importantly, where she could see them.

"Well, if you're sure."

"I am. Thank you for lunch and for showing me the exhibition."

"Both were my son's idea." But she sounded gratified, and Simone got the sense of a caring woman beneath the haughty facade. Given time she could probably break through to that woman, she thought. Not that she'd be at the palace for long enough.

All the more reason to use the time well, she thought as her hostess adjusted her abaya and showed Simone the way to the main courtyard. She made sure her headdress shaded most of her face before stepping outside.

It had been a long day and it wasn't over yet, Markaz reflected as he stepped out of his office onto the mosaic-floored veranda running the length of this pavilion. Dealing with the police who'd made no more progress with their investigations had taken up half the morning. Then there was that nonsense with young Bibi smuggling her boyfriend into her room. Boyfriend? They were both little more than children. He hoped that having the police pretend to arrest young Abdl had taught them a lesson.

Markaz had nothing against young love. But Bibi's family had entrusted him with her care. Having to tell them she'd gotten herself into trouble would be a poor way to repay their trust.

Lying about taking the boy to her room had fueled Markaz's anger. When he was five his beloved grandfather had been terminally ill and the adults had tried to shield him with lies. Learning the truth too late to say goodbye, he'd been devastated. He'd hated deception ever since, as Natalie had found to her cost.

Thinking of the desperate way Bibi had kissed Abdl before they were separated, Markaz felt something else twist inside him. Jealousy? he wondered, but dismissed the thought as soon as it arose. He'd never been that innocent in his whole life. And certainly never so much in love that nothing else mattered.

Was that his problem? For as long as he could recall his life had been ruled by duty. Marrying Natalie had been his only digression from the prescribed path, and look how that had turned out? He'd never forgiven her for not telling him about her undercover work, wondering to the end whether she'd really loved him or had married him out of duty.

He could hardly fault her for that, he thought. Much as he valued truth, he also understood duty better than most people. And now she was dead, he was surprised to find himself grieving for her. Not for a love that had withered long ago, but because no one deserved such a cruel end.

The arrangements to return her body to America were already being made, and he planned to fly there to attend her funeral. Now he decided to plant an olive tree in the grounds of Al-Qasr as a memorial, recognizing that her last act had been to serve the country she'd never learned to love.

From the veranda he stepped into a vast courtyard once used for gatherings such as dancing and contests. Now it was deserted, with only the sound of the fountain playing at its center and faint music emanating from within the palace. He pulled in a deep breath. Peaceful moments like these were rare, and it wouldn't be long before Fayed came to summon him to his next appointment.

As he stepped out into the sunlight, he barely noticed his guards detach themselves from the shadows and follow at a discreet distance. Their presence was as natural to him as the breeze stirring the sand in the courtyard, and no more remarkable. The absence of the guards would have been more noticeable.

Then he saw her.

How he knew the veiled figure was Simone, he wasn't sure. Something about the way she walked in the unaccustomed garments, or the bold angle of her head, so different from the women of his country. But he knew.

Odd that he should have been thinking about love when she appeared. Ever since he kissed her—or more accurately, she kissed him—she'd haunted his thoughts.

For the last two nights he'd lain awake, preoccupied by the feel of her in his arms, the softness and the core of strength. A mouth all sweetness as she took and gave equally. The compulsion to taste her again had left him tossing and turning.

"*Ahlan*," she greeted him in Arabic, startling him. He

hadn't heard her come closer. Too deafened by his own thoughts. Evidently she didn't know it was customary to wait until addressed by the sheikh, before speaking.

Deciding to overlook the transgression, he returned the greeting, "*Ahlan beek.* Walk with me."

She inclined her head, her expression hidden beneath the abaya. "As you wish, Your Highness."

"It was Markaz the other evening."

She glanced at the guards. "We were alone then."

He shrugged. "We are alone now." As alone as he managed to be most of the time.

She fell into step beside him. "Have the police made any progress?"

The scent of jasmine drifted to him, taking him back to his dream. He didn't want to talk about murder and mayhem. What he wanted to discuss didn't bear thinking about. "No," he said shortly.

"You seem angry with me. Why, when I've done all you asked?"

Even kissed him. Her veil should have saved him from such thoughts, but being able to see only her expressive eyes made her mouth seem like a secret pleasure, more tantalizing for being a hint behind a layer of gauze.

His anger was at himself for having no more restraint than young Abdl. "You shouldn't be out here alone."

Her gesture indicated the guards posted at intervals around the courtyard. "I'm well guarded."

"Possibly by the traitor in the palace."

"Then the risks are the same anywhere within the walls."

He made an impatient sound. "You have an answer for everything."

* * *

Not quite everything, Simone thought. What was the answer to the sudden fast beating of her heart as soon as she saw him enter the courtyard? To the heat boiling through her? Blaming the layers of clothing didn't help. She'd felt comfortable until he appeared.

She would be comfortable again, she vowed silently. She had to be. "Thank you for asking Princess Norah to show me the embroidery," she said, deliberately aiming for neutral ground.

"Afwan." You're welcome. "Did you choose a design to use in your business?"

"I can do that?"

"Didn't my mother tell you? I couldn't think of a better reward."

"And I couldn't ask for one." Excitement vibrated in her voice. He wanted her to have the right to reproduce one of the unique designs as a gift. For her service to Nazaar, not to him, she reminded herself. It wasn't personal. Norah must have forgotten to tell her. "I'll need time to decide, but it's a wonderful gift. *Shukran.* Thank you. Although I did little to deserve it."

"Not little at all. Without you, Natalie's body could have lain in the desert for days. We'd never have known what had happened to her."

Across the courtyard she saw Fayed approaching with two other men in palace uniform. Instantly Markaz's guards fell into formation with them. Seeing them, Markaz tensed visibly. Duty, she guessed. Did the demands on him never stop?

She wondered at her urge to tell them to go away and leave the sheikh alone. With her, came the unwanted postscript. Just as well her expression was veiled, hiding the desperation accompanying the thought. He made her want far more than was good for her. Or even possible to have.

Fayed salaamed and reminded the sheikh of an imminent appointment, while the attendants waited stiffly. The men paid her no attention, but this time she was glad. Her focus was riveted by one man in particular. Dark-eyed, thin and bearded, he was a double of the other guards except for one sloping shoulder slightly higher than the other and a look that reminded her of her father. He and his half brother had shared the same mother, so a family resemblance was likely.

Yusef al Hasa? It was all she could do not to blurt out the name in case he went by a different one now. But even allowing for the passage of time, her mother's description fit. Unable to see his wrist under his dishdasha, Simone couldn't check for a tattoo of a coiled snake, but she sensed she'd found him. If it was Yusef, how would he react when she revealed who she was?

With grave formality Markaz took his leave, his mind clearly already on his official duties. She didn't demur when he assigned one of the guards to escort her back to her quarters, only regretting that the chosen man wasn't Yusef.

Chapter 7

When Simone returned to the women's quarters, Amal was away at her studies, but had left a message with Bibi that she would be back in two hours. This gave Simone plenty of time to think about how to approach Yusef.

The task wasn't as simple as it looked. In Australia she would have asked her escort to tell her the other man's name, then picked up a house phone and called him. Here the rules were stricter. A woman contacting a man she didn't know could easily be taken the wrong way.

How did people live under so many rules without going crazy? The sooner the sheikh brought in the rest of his reforms, the better. Not that she'd be around to see them, she reminded herself. He was as keen to see the last of her as she was to leave.

She didn't like thinking ego was her problem, but had to face facts. She'd wanted him to react as strongly to her as she'd done at seeing him step out into the courtyard. Such a nerve-jolting, stomach-clenching sensation had no business being one-sided.

The flowing *sirwall* pants hampered her attempt to pace around the living room of her suite. What if the response *was* one-sided? She'd live. A Western woman with a life of her own didn't turn to mush over a man, even one as prepossessing as Sheikh Markaz.

No, an independent woman dismissed him from her mind and focused on what was important: arranging a meeting with Yusef, and taking care of her own business. With nothing to be done about her half uncle right now, that left her business affairs.

Hunting out the universal remote, she pressed buttons until a panel slid back revealing a computer screen set into a wall. Settling herself comfortably on a velvet chaise longue with a wireless keyboard across her lap, she worked through the connections and logged on to her Web site. For the next hour she answered e-mails and processed orders. They would be handled in Australia by Drew Wyatt, Simone's business partner. Markaz would probably be scandalized that her associate was a man, but Simone had known Drew since college and he was like a brother to her. He could make a computer sit up and beg, and he had made the Web site more professional and eye-catching.

E-mailing him some notes on what actions needed taking, Simone let her hands still on the keyboard. Hard to believe she was effectively running a business in Australia from a harem in Nazaar, but that's what she was doing.

Finally closing the connection and putting the keyboard to one side, she picked up the glossy catalog Princess Norah had given her and immediately started imagining how each of the designs would look on her Web site. What an attraction they'd be. Something no other heirloom embroidery site could offer. Markaz had said she could have the right to the design of her choice as her reward. Choosing which one to feature was the challenge.

She was engrossed in the catalog when Amal tripped into the suite, her arms full of books and her pretty face flushed. "You're looking at my class's star pupil," she announced.

"Congratulations." Feeling a rush of warmth for the other woman, Simone got up and hugged her.

"What have you been up to?" Amal asked when they'd exhausted the news of her high grades, and a servant had brought them glasses of chilled fruit juice.

When Simone told her about lunching with Princess Norah, she made a face. "Was she as hard to get along with as usual?"

"Then the problem isn't just me?"

Amal shook her head. "Markaz has only to glance at a woman to earn Norah's displeasure. I think she fears losing him the way she lost her husband and son. She wasn't so prickly before the assassinations," Amal added. "When it happened she was away at the family's desert retreat, and blames herself for not being at Sheikh Kemal's side."

Regretting her harsh judgment of the princess, Simone sipped the juice thoughtfully. "Such a terrible experience would change anybody. She was actually quite nice when she forgot to be disapproving." She explained about being shown the embroidery exhibition, and the sheikh's offer to give her the rights to the design of her choice for her business.

"You've made quite an impression on both of them," Amal enthused. "Maybe Princess Norah has good reason to worry about you."

The meaning was clear and Simone felt heat travel up

her neck and into her face. "I'm sure you're wrong. Either way, it's impossible. We're from two different worlds."

Amal wasn't ready to give up. "So was Markaz's father, and Markaz himself. Both chose foreign wives."

"Yes, and look how that turned out."

"I met Natalie a few times," Amal said thoughtfully. "Unlike you, she hated everything about Nazaari life, except Markaz, of course."

"How do you know I don't hate it?" As far as Simone was concerned, the jury was still out.

"You don't, do you?"

The young royal sounded so distressed that Simone was forced to shake her head. "No. Some things are difficult, like being confined to one part of the palace, and having to hide under concealing clothes."

"They're for your protection, because of the circumstances bringing you here," Amal reminded her. "Today I drove myself to the university, and attended my class unveiled."

"Yee ha," Simone said dryly. Chiding herself for taking out her frustration on Amal, she said, "Sorry, I realize they're big steps to you. But I've gone where I pleased and worn what I liked for most of my adult life."

"Has the freedom made you happy?"

How to answer honestly? "I'm happy enough. I have a good life, plenty of friends and work that I love."

"What about a husband and children?"

"In time. You're hardly a poster child for marriage yourself."

"I will be as soon as I finish my degree."

This was news to Simone. "You're engaged?"

It was Amal's turn to color. "I have an understanding with a man from my own province. Gibran is studying psychology and we plan to set up a practice together after we're married."

Again a feeling very like jealousy assailed Simone. Amal glowed with happiness. So much for pitying the downtrodden women of Nazaar.

"I hope it works out for you," she said sincerely.

"For you, too." Collecting her books together, Amal rose. "I have an essay to write, so I'll see you at dinner later."

"Before you go, can I ask you something? I want to talk to one of Markaz's household guards. How do I go about contacting him?"

Amal shifted her books more comfortably in her arms. "Why would you want to speak to another man, when you've caught Markaz's eye?"

Impossible to explain without saying too much about Yusef's past. "I haven't caught Markaz's eye. He feels responsible for my safety. Besides, I only want to talk to this man. I think my parents knew him before they went to Australia."

Amal sat down again. "Tell me all you know of him."

There wasn't much. But with her experience of palace life, Amal filled in the gaps. "If I have the right man, he's Omar Zirhan who joined Markaz's guard four months ago."

"Only four months?" Thinking she knew why he used another name, Simone wondered what he'd been doing before joining the palace guard.

The question was quickly answered. "He was an unemployed security guard who saved the sheikh's life by driving away a car filled with explosives seconds before Markaz arrived for an official engagement. Luckily for both men, the car didn't explode. In gratitude, Markaz gave him a place in the household guard."

Simone's eyes misted. Good news for her mother at last. "He's a hero?"

"A modest one who insists he did nothing extraordinary. If I'm right, he's usually posted outside the hall of justice at this time."

Remembering the room she'd seen with Norah earlier, Simone became excited. "Can we see him now?"

"It isn't appropriate for a woman to approach a man and start a conversation."

"Then how—"

Amal lifted a hand. "There are ways. Since I'm known to be committed to Gibran, I can take the guard a cold drink without setting tongues wagging. Having someone accompany me is seemly. You can talk to him while I prepare the drink."

As soon as she saw him outside the justice hall Simone recognized the man as the guard she'd seen earlier. He looked pleased to see Amal. She made a habit of doing good deeds, Simone gathered as they carried a tray containing a sweating pitcher of juice, a glass and a piece of baklava to the guard's post. "You're a lifesaver," he said as she placed the tray on a parapet. He didn't even look at Simone hiding behind her veil.

"Amal tells me you're a hero," she said in Arabic, keeping her eyes downcast.

"Sima is my cousin," Amal supplied over her shoulder as she poured the drink.

His expression was sullen. "Don't believe everything Amal tells you, Sima. She enjoys drama."

"But you did save the sheikh's life," Simone persisted.

"So the story goes."

He wouldn't budge. Instinct told Simone there was

more here than a modest hero. She wished she could tell him who she was, but until she knew more about his circumstances, she had to do this Amal's way. "Some friends in Australia were asking for news of you," she said.

His gaze darkened. "I don't know anyone in Australia."

Odd. "What about Ali and Sara al Hasa?"

He frowned and shook his head. "Never heard of them. What's keeping that juice, Amal? A man could die of thirst at his post."

The young royal gave him the glass and he lifted it to his mouth. He drank deeply, the sleeve of his dishdasha sliding to his elbow.

A tattoo of a snake encircled his right wrist.

Excitement gripped Simone, but she checked it. Something was wrong. Why did he deny knowing her parents, his own family? Saving the sheikh's life proved he no longer sided with the rebels, so what did he have to hide?

Amal was too kindhearted, Markaz thought as he watched the scene from his office window. Behind him the rooms were in darkness, but he didn't turn on a light, partly because Amal would be embarrassed that he'd seen her kind act, but also because he wanted to preserve his night vision.

He'd ordered Omar Zirhan posted within sight of his office, not as he'd let people think, to reward him for heroism, but to keep an eye on him. Ever since the sheikh's security people had learned that the only DNA found on the explosive in the van was Zirhan's, he'd been under surveillance.

Not much was known about him before his heroic deed, and that of itself was unusual. In Nazaar, family was everything. Zirhan was different. As far as the records showed, his line started and ended with himself. What details the sheikh's people had uncovered were sparse. Zirhan was an orphan raised in Raisa at a school for homeless boys. He'd worked as a security guard at the largest souk in the city, but had been let go. He'd said it was because of personality clashes with his boss.

Keen to see him rewarded, the people had petitioned the sheikh to hire him. Wanting answers, Markaz had played along. Only Fayed and Hamal and a handful of trusted staff knew about his suspicions.

Fayed and Hamal thought Markaz was taking an unnecessary risk by hiring Zirhan. But how else could he find out what was going on? He'd ordered the man's room bugged and his movements watched, but no results so far.

Watching the scene outside the justice hall, he hated to think of Amal being involved. As fast as the thought arose, he dismissed it. He'd known her all his life, and she was as sweet as she appeared. She was well suited to her chosen social work, loving people and trusting them until proven wrong. Befriending a loner like Zirhan was entirely in her character.

What about the woman with her? Veiled and in shadow, she was hard to make out. Then she moved and he knew. Simone. She was also a stranger who'd come into his life through a good deed, albeit with a better pedigree than Zirhan. That didn't mean Markaz should trust her.

He saw her talking to the guard who responded dismissively. Simone was veiled, but by her posture, Markaz saw she was upset. Plotting? he wondered.

She'd said she was looking for a relative, but the name she'd given Markaz wasn't Omar Zirhan, and the guard didn't behave like a long-lost relative now.

Only when Markaz's nails dug into his palms did he unclench his hands, realizing how much he wanted her to be innocent. Needed her to be on his side. Needed her a lot closer than that, if he was honest.

Getting soft? he asked himself. How he hated the mistrust the rebels sowed in his kingdom. They must be rooted out once and for all, even if it meant heads had to roll. The thought of Simone meeting such an end made him feel ill, but he knew he'd give the order himself if it brought peace to his country.

His own feelings were irrelevant.

That didn't mean he could deny their existence, and frustration seethed through him. Simone affected him in ways no woman had done since his marriage. The short time he'd known her didn't seem to matter. The connection had been instant and powerful. It was working on him still. Clouding his judgment? Yes, if he wasn't careful.

Spinning on his heel, he returned to his office, turned on the lights and pulled his laptop toward him. He was staring at a legal document without really seeing it when Fayed came in. "Working late, Markaz?"

"Brooding."

Fayed eased himself into a chair that creaked under his massive frame. "Anything I can do to help?"

Markaz closed the laptop. "Having you to talk to helps. If Omar Zirhan is a traitor, why doesn't he act? What's he waiting for?"

"Perhaps for you to move the household to Karama." The desert city had been the royal family's winter home for generations.

The censure in Fayed's tone wearied Markaz. "We've gone over this before. The people expect me to conduct the majlis, the sheikh's court, at Karama at this time every year. I will not be kept away by nameless threats. What can Zirhan do there that he can't do here?"

"Only the rebels know their intentions. All I know is that the desert lodge is less well protected than the palace."

"Then you're convinced he's one of them?"

Fayed frowned. "What other explanation is there?"

"It could be as the man said, he was in the right place at the right time."

"That is one aspect we agree on."

Leaving only the reason in dispute. Markaz stood up and flattened his palms against his desk. "The household will move to Karama as usual."

Fayed climbed to his feet, the effort belying the speed he could employ when needed. "As Your Highness wishes. What will you do about the Australian woman?"

Markaz rolled his neck to one side then the other. "She'll accompany us." He'd shocked his old friend, he saw. "If there is a conspiracy, I prefer to know who we're dealing with. If she and Zirhan are in league, we have them both where we can watch them. If we neutralize them, they could be replaced by others we may not identify in time."

Fayed inclined his head in acceptance of the sheikh's logic. "With your permission, I'll brief Hamal."

Markaz smiled. "Do that. And don't worry, I haven't lost my head over Simone." If he was stretching the truth, he was glad Fayed didn't call him on it.

Simone prowled around the terrace of her suite, the abaya swirling around her legs. By night the view of the palace grounds and the sparkling city beyond looked romantic, but she was in no mood to appreciate it. "He *is* Yusef al Hasa, I'd swear to it."

"Then why does he call himself Omar Zirhan?"

Simone paused, weighing the risk against her conviction that she could trust Amal. "Can I tell you a secret?"

She explained about Yusef's relationship to her mother, and her own belief that he had changed his name to hide his rebel past and start a new life. "Why would he save the sheikh's life unless he has changed?" she concluded.

Amal nodded. "You have a good point, but I have a question, too. If he has left his past behind for good reason, why do you insist that he acknowledge your relationship?"

"My mother's state of health won't improve until she knows that the family member she left behind is safe and well."

"Isn't it enough to tell her that you've seen him, and can assure her all is well?"

The hem of Simone's abaya caught on a chair and she tugged it free. "I can't be sure he's really Yusef al Hasa until I hear it from him."

"Even if Omar Zirhan isn't your father's half brother after all?"

She'd already considered that. "If he isn't, I'll keep looking."

Amal looked down. "That may be difficult. The royal household moves to Karama at the end of this week so Markaz can preside over the winter majlis, the sheikh's court."

Simone began to pace again. She hadn't anticipated this. "He'll probably send me back to Australia before you leave. That doesn't give me much time to work on Yusef or Omar. The only way he'll admit his real identity is if I tell him mine."

"You mustn't for your own safety in case Natalie's killer is still looking for you."

The parapet blocked Simone's pacing and she swung around. "I have to take the risk. If Yusef knows we're related, he won't hurt me. I'll wait until Markaz is ready to send me away." This thought brought its own portion of distress, but she thrust it aside. "I'll confront Yusef when it's too late for him to do anything about it. All I want is for him to acknowledge his relationship to my family. I'm also going to take a photo of him for her, with or without his consent. Is that asking so much?"

Amal clasped her hands together. "I suppose not. Be careful, please."

Simone had no wish to court additional danger, so she nodded. "I will."

She should have guessed that the sheikh would have his own agenda. Next morning while she and Amal were eating breakfast, Simone received a summons to his office.

She'd been in the courtyard outside, but not in his inner sanctum. *Office* was too slight a word to describe the grandeur of the room. Priceless Persian carpets softened acres of marble floor, while stone columns soared to a vaulted ceiling, dividing the ballroom-sized room into working and conference areas.

A surprise was an imposing baronial fireplace bordered by timber bookshelves filled with leather-bound volumes arranged slightly unevenly, which suggested they were not only for show. In front of the fireplace a pair of sofas upholstered in dark green leather were separated by a bronze-based table with a stone top. Fayed led her to this area while the sheikh completed some paperwork at a desk the size of a double bed.

Not a useful comparison, considering her blood had started to pump harder as soon as she approached him. In an open-necked white shirt with the sleeves rolled back over tanned forearms, he even sat regally. His dark hair gleamed in a ray of sunlight from the window. Recalling how springy his hair felt, she curled her fingers into her palms to keep herself steady.

He acknowledged her arrival with a nod, and kept working as Fayed showed her to the conference area, salaamed and left. From where she sat, the sheikh's shoulders looked tense and his face was set in a scowl. Either the papers holding his attention were depressing him, or she was.

She couldn't believe he regretted kissing her the night she arrived. Not when the sparks had been so powerful and undeniably mutual.

Her breathing tangled as Markaz joined her, taking a seat on the opposite sofa and resting his hands on his knees. "Did Amal tell you that the court moves to Karama at the end of the week?" he asked without any of the usual polite exchanges.

There could be only one reason. He was glad to be rid of her. Her throat started to ache. "Yes. I assume it means you're sending me back to Australia."

His stern visage didn't lighten. "I thought about it."

The hope rekindled. "And?"

How would she respond if Markaz said he was keeping her under surveillance after watching her make contact with a suspected rebel? He resisted the temptation to ask. The truth would come out soon enough. Looking so doe-eyed and apparently confused by his aloofness, she made him want to abandon caution and sweep her into his arms. Desire flamed through him like a lit torch. Her abaya was loose around her shoulders. Her unveiled mouth taunted him, all remembered pleasure and future promise. If she was involved with the rebels, she was one hell of a secret weapon.

The thought sobered him enough to keep him on his side of the low table. But not to douse the flames. He'd have to do that the hard way through force of will, until he learned the truth about her and Zirhan.

"I decided you're safer under royal protection," he said, breaking the long silence.

"I'm going with you to Karama? Into the desert?"

He couldn't believe her delight was faked, and hoped that it wasn't because he'd handed her the opportunity to harm him or his government. He'd soon learn the truth about that as well.

In the meantime, he would keep her at arm's length. Although from the way she affected him, he suspected it wouldn't be nearly far enough.

Chapter 8

Simone didn't mind traveling with the royal women, one faceless veiled figure among many, as long as she got to see the country beyond Raisa. So far she'd only visited Al-Qasr, but this time they were traveling to Nazaar's second largest city of Karama, two hundred miles away. Her father's birthplace and the home of her ancestors.

Now as Simone watched the savanna country roll by dotted with villages and herds of camels, she wondered how her father had felt as a teenager, leaving behind everything he knew to try his luck in the capital. Simone hoped he would be proud of her for retracing his steps, taking his memory back with her.

She was glad to be traveling with Amal and Bibi, relieved not to find herself sharing a car with Markaz's mother. But Princess Norah was alone in the car directly ahead of them, while the sheikh was in the lead vehicle.

With the rest of the household having gone ahead to prepare, they made quite a procession.

"Karama is very much like Raisa Palace, except for being smaller with no separate women's quarters, so you must be careful about wearing your veil when you leave your room," Amal cautioned her.

Elated at hearing she wouldn't be shut away in a separate part of the royal lodge, Simone was disappointed at the prospect of being veiled most of the time. At least at Raisa, she could dispense with the abaya within the women's quarters. Now it looked as if she'd be stuck with it.

The other women didn't seem to mind, but they'd grown up with the wretched things. Simone missed the freedom of light clothing and bare feet, and the wind in her hair. Telling herself the inconvenience was a small price to pay for her safety didn't help as much as it should.

"Why are we stopping?" she asked, her heart lurching as the limousine pulled up as if responding to her thought.

"We've reached al Faransi, where we have lunch," Amal answered.

The driver opened the door for them, the heat making Simone reel as she stepped out into it. They had arrived at a retreat built around an oasis with the beautiful Nazaar Mountains as a backdrop, and the towering dunes of the Lost Quarter—the true desert—visible in the distance. "Is that a zoo?" she asked, disbelief in her tone as she looked beyond the cluster of low, white-painted buildings.

Amal nodded. "*Faransi* literally means *of France*. At one time this was a training center for French foreign legionnaires. They left behind a number of animals that were once mascots. When Sheikh Kemal established this place, he included the animals in a zoo along with many other exhibits. Now it's a popular tourist attraction."

That accounted for the many vehicles and a tourist coach parked near the main building. "Will there be time to look around before we move on?" she asked.

Amal gracefully adjusted her abaya. "Markaz usually meets with the present owners to discuss their concerns, so we'll be here for a couple of hours. I hope you don't mind if I wait inside while you look around. I've seen the zoo several times."

"I'm not dragging around some boring zoo, either," Bibi insisted. "I'll stay inside with you, Amal."

Cheered by the prospect of a little solitude, Simone inclined her head in agreement. "I'll be fine by myself."

"You must take a guard with you," Amal insisted.

So much for time alone. On the other hand, Yusef, or Omar as he called himself, was also in the party. Maybe he could be persuaded to escort her. "Good idea," Simone said.

Their lunch had been set up in a separate pavilion away from the public buildings. As usual, the men dined in one room and the women in another, making Simone wonder how romance ever managed to blossom.

Somehow it did. Bibi and her Abdl were an example. Perhaps the thrill of the forbidden added to the allure. Simone didn't like to think how important a glimpse of Markaz had become to her.

A gauze curtain across an archway separated the rooms. When it billowed aside she saw him talking with a group of men.

He looked up and caught her watching him. Her heart backflipped. He shouldn't know her from the other veiled women, but his gaze found her with the precision of a heat-seeking missile.

The slight curve of his sensuous mouth was enough to

send fire pulsing through her. From the desert air, she told herself, although she'd felt cool a second before.

Lunch included platters of traditional flat bread, mounds of glistening rice and chunks of chicken cooked in a spicy sauce. The usual fresh salads, fruits and pastries completed the meal. Afterward the other women were content to laze on the low, cushioned banquets and talk, but Simone was determined to look around.

"I need to walk off some of the rich food," she told Amal.

Her plan to ask Yusef to be her escort was thwarted when another guard attached himself to her as soon as she stepped outside. "Where would you like to go, Princess?" he asked respectfully in Arabic.

"The zoo, but I'm fine on my own. It isn't far away," she said in kind.

He didn't answer but fell into step beside her, making it clear she wouldn't be going anywhere unescorted.

The zoo was much larger than it had appeared at first. Simone wouldn't have time to see more than the closest exhibits. Much of the zoo looked to be open range areas, sheltering herds of antelope, as well as the rare Nazaaran gazelle. She was also fascinated to see the Arabian oryx, a desert animal her father had told her about, with large straight horns and striking black and white markings. The zoo claimed to have the world's largest desert-based aquarium with sea lions, penguins and fifty species of fish.

Already feeling light-headed from the heat, she chose the aquarium, unable to resist the appeal of penguins in the desert. Only a few people were around and none were entering the aquarium. Injecting authority into her voice she said, "According to the map, this is the only entrance, so I'll be fine in here. Wait for me outside."

Her escort saluted. "As you wish, Princess."

She was getting the hang of this royal business, she decided as she stepped into the dim coolness to find herself among tanks containing sharks, stingrays, tropical fish and jewel-colored corals. With the aquarium to herself, she let her veil dangle to one side, ready to be pulled across her face if anyone came in.

Breathing freely at last she wandered between the tanks until she found the promised penguin exhibit.

The contrast between the desert outside and the imitation seashore in front of her made her smile. She leaned against a wall of artificial rock, watching the knee-high creatures at play. Back home in Port Lincoln she'd often seen little penguins fishing along the shore of the Great Australian Bight.

Suddenly a wave of homesickness swept over her and she gripped the rock wall to steady herself. What on earth was she doing thousands of miles from her birthplace, watching penguins on the fringe of the Nazaari desert? Was the appeal really the prospect of seeing her father's country, or of being with Markaz? Either way, she was as out of place as these penguins. The sooner she established Yusef's true identity and headed home, the better.

Trying to imagine picking up the threads of her life wasn't as easy as it should have been. Whenever she logged on to her Web site and saw the design she'd chosen as her reward from Markaz, she'd be reminded of him. She stifled a laugh. Who was she kidding? Most of what they'd shared was in her head. He'd kissed her exactly once, and she'd spent only a handful of hours in his company. Some romance.

Unsettled by her thoughts, she pushed away from the stone wall. Time to rejoin the women. Then she tensed, instinctively reaching for the veil and securing it over her face. But she was too late. Lost in thought, she hadn't seen the man watching her intently from across the penguin enclosure. As he started toward her she recognized Business Suit.

She hadn't seen him since he'd pursued her at Al-Qasr, but his features were etched on her brain. This time there was no Fayed to rescue her, and the guard was outside and out of earshot.

Business Suit had to cut around the penguin enclosure, giving her a few seconds to slip away between the tanks. A huge electric-blue Napoleon wrasse watched her, its humped head resting against the glass as it waited to be fed from above. That gave her an idea.

Her frantic search located a narrow metal ladder in the shadows at the back of the tank. Hampered by her clothing, she climbed up to a small metal platform where a bucket of baitfish stood ready for a keeper to distribute among the tank's occupants. From the way the wrasse and a horde of smaller fish speared toward her, it must have been close to their feeding time.

Her heart hammered as she looked down and saw Business Suit come into view, his features distorted by the water and the curving glass. He looked around then pounded a fist against the tank in frustration. The vibrations matched her racing heartbeat.

When he started around the tank, she picked up the bucket of fish and tipped it into the water. On cue the Napoleon wrasse and the other fish swarmed closer, scooping up the food. Staying carefully in the shadows, she saw Business Suit look up. When all he saw was an aquarium employee at work, he moved swiftly toward the ramp leading to the exit. A flash of sunlight indicated the door opening then closing again.

Her ragged breathing ruffled her veil. She'd done it, outwitted him a second time. Then she was disturbed by a shout. "Hey, what are you doing? Only employees are allowed up there."

Checking that her veil was secure, she clambered down and apologized in Arabic to the angry keeper whose job she'd usurped. He chastised her verbally as a stupid woman and she didn't try to defend herself. The tirade would buy her time while Business Suit moved away.

With a last effusive apology, she headed for the entrance and was thankful to see the guard waiting for her. In response to her questions, he assured her he hadn't seen anything unusual. Yes, he'd seen a man come out of the aquarium, but assumed that he worked for the zoo. She didn't try to explain. "Take me to Sheikh Markaz. I have vital information for him that can't wait."

"He gave me orders not to be disturbed."

"Then I'll make my own way." Keeping a lookout for Business Suit, she marched ahead of the protesting guard back to the pavilion where they'd had lunch. The women were drinking coffee and talking among themselves. Ignoring their startled looks, she pulled aside the gauze curtain separating them from the men.

Their murmurs told her what a sight she must present, pursued by a guard, bedraggled from climbing around in the aquarium and with the sleeves of her galabia soaked from feeding the fish. Lounging on low banquets, the men were drinking from bell-shaped cups and talking in lowered tones. She ignored their startled reactions and sailed down the room to where Markaz occupied the seat of honor beside his host.

"Your Highness, we need to talk."

Markaz murmured something to his host that she didn't

catch and uncoiled from the low seat to loom over her. "What is the meaning of this intrusion?"

Lowering her voice, she said, "Business Suit followed us here. He almost caught me in the aquarium."

"Go to my car. I'll deal with you there." To Fayed hovering beside him, he said more loudly, "Take her out of here."

With her feet barely touching the floor, she was hustled to Markaz's limousine and thrust unceremoniously into the back. The click of locks engaging, and the privacy panel slamming shut sounded like the closing of prison gates.

Her face burned as she snatched off her veil, thinking of the cruel and unusual things she would like to do to Markaz. Hadn't he heard her? She was in danger and that meant so was he. Locking her in his car wasn't going to help if Business Suit was still out there. Gradually her burn subsided to a simmer. She was also as protected as she could be for now.

Screened by the tinted windows that Amal had told her earlier were bulletproof, she could only sit back and wait. Accessing the vehicle's bar, she helped herself to a glass of sparkling water.

She took a deep swallow of the drink. Wandering around the aquarium on her own ranked near the top of the crazy scale. But this whole situation was making her crazy. She'd come to Nazaar to help her mother, not get involved in a plot against the country's ruler, far less to fall in…in lust with him.

Markaz pushed all her female buttons in the worst way. And being caught up in the plot meant she couldn't get away from him. Nor could she do anything about her feelings. If he'd been anyone else, she could have indulged in a hot and heavy, no-holds-barred fling and gotten him out of her system. The way he affected her, she doubted it would be that simple. In any case a fling with the sheikh of sheikhs was out of the question.

Frustration made her search the doors for a way out, but the car was securely locked. By barging in on the men, she'd flouted all kinds of protocol. Locking her in the car was probably the least Markaz was expected to do.

Cradling the drink in both hands, she seethed silently. If he'd only paid attention instead of pulling rank, his men could have gone after Business Suit. While the coffee ritual went on, he was getting away.

She started as the door opened, but Markaz slid in beside her. The driver closed the door behind him. Moments later she felt a smooth acceleration. The motorcade was under way again.

The sheikh had seen her reaction, and his features darkened in a scowl. "The time to be frightened was before you went off on your own. The guard told me you ordered him to wait outside the aquarium."

Her anger rose to meet his, although some of it was at herself for the way her pulse drummed as he swung to face her. "There's only one entrance. I thought it was safe enough," she said.

He looked set to explode. "What you thought doesn't matter. Had you let the guard do his job, he might have caught your assailant and this would be over."

She tightened her grip on her glass so she wouldn't throw the contents over him. "You'd like that, wouldn't you? Then you'd be rid of me for good."

"You think that's what I want?"

"The way you spoke to me in front of the men, ordering Fayed to hustle me out to your car, speaks for itself."

"There is another interpretation."

"Sure, that I'm a lowly woman who has to be put in her

place because she dares to stick her nose into men's affairs."

A nerve jumped along his jaw and he bunched his dishdasha in clenched fists as if to stop himself lashing out. "Will you be silent?"

She thrust the glass into the bar, afraid that if she held on to it she *would* throw it at him. "I won't be silent. I don't appreciate being treated like dirt for trying to tell you something that might save our lives. Damn it, I was terrified out of my wits, and all you could do was order me out of your sight."

He grabbed her flailing hands, frowning as he felt the trembling she couldn't control. "I didn't treat you like dirt. I got you out of there before you said too much."

Aware of heat flooding through her from him, she shook her head. "What?"

"One of the men having coffee with us is a suspected rebel. He could have tipped your Business Suit off that our party intended to stop here on our way to Karama."

Her voice dropped to a whisper. "You think this was a trap?"

"Very possibly. The suspect is distantly related to the owner of al Faransi. Sheikh Aziz was one of my father's oldest friends, which is why I patronize his establishment. I don't think he knows what his relative is involved in. Aziz seemed surprised to see him here today."

"Like me and Business Suit," she said, her fingers spasming in his grasp. "When he showed up in the aquarium…"

"It's all right," the sheikh soothed, cutting her off. "You're safe now."

Her control snapped. "It wasn't my safety I was worried about."

She hadn't meant to tell him that. Surrounded by soldiers and a bodyguard the size of a mountain, Markaz would probably find her concern for him laughable. Instead warmth flashed in his gaze. "Looks like we have more than one problem."

She tried to pull her hands away but he held on, so she strived for lightness in her tone. "No problem. I just don't want anything happening to you."

His fingers wove distracting patterns around hers. "Because?"

"This country needs you and your reform plans."

"And you, Sima? What do you need?"

His soft use of the name she'd adopted in his harem, the same nickname used so lovingly by her parents, increased her tremors. Not with fear, although she wouldn't name any other cause even in her mind. "I need this to be over."

The doubts, the yearnings Markaz heard in her voice were echoed in his thoughts. When she'd burst in on the men, he'd wanted to take her in his arms and soothe her fears. Only knowing he could be betraying her to Aziz's relative had kept his hands at his sides. Watching Fayed hustle her away on his own orders, he'd felt like a monster.

"The danger will be over soon," he promised. "Hamal and his men searched the complex without finding Business Suit, but I had Aziz's relative arrested. He'll be taken to police headquarters at Raisa, and may lead us to his associates."

Her abaya had drifted back over her shoulders. He tucked both of her hands into one of his so he could brush the strands of coppery hair out of her eyes. She made a stunning brunette, but he missed her unique golden beauty.

She knew, he thought, seeing panic flare in her gaze. She knew because she felt the connection, too. When they were in the same space, and sometimes when they weren't, it wove between them like an invisible thread. But why the panic? She was safe from the man she called Business Suit for the moment. So something else had provoked her fear. Markaz hoped it wasn't him.

He couldn't help himself. He had to know. Using their joined hands for leverage, he pulled her toward him and locked his mouth on hers, his breath sighing out as he finally, finally let himself taste her. He'd wanted to kiss her again since the first night in the New York suite.

If she'd shown the slightest resistance he would have pulled back. Although his genes urged him to take and plunder, he disciplined himself to test her response, letting his lips quest lightly over hers.

When they parted for him, he felt joy leap inside him and deepened the kiss, releasing her hands so he could pull her closer. Her heart pounded against his chest.

He felt her hands slide around his back, her splayed fingers hot through his clothes. Hotter still the way her mouth shaped itself to his demands. He was glad to see she kept her eyes open as they kissed. Good. He wanted her in no doubt about who was giving her such pleasure.

Not that it was one-sided. As her fingers tangled in his hair his whole being thrummed like the deep mellow notes of the oud, not for nothing called the king of musical instruments, until it was moot who was playing who. Her touch made his neck and scalp seem like the most erogenous zones in his body, although they were getting steadily increasing competition from the more usual parts.

Testing her mouth with the tip of his tongue, he heard her breath catch. Such a chaste sound and so at odds with the way her tongue danced around his. He closed his teeth lightly around her lower lip. Her sigh became a faint moan and her lashes drooped.

Lifting his head, he gazed at her, his chest tightening as he saw her tongue dart out to moisten her lips. Her head had fallen back against the leather cushions and she lay across the seat under him. He'd actually started to move his robes out of the way when he realized what he was doing.

He stopped, although everything in him urged him on. What was he *doing*? He should be demanding answers about her involvement with Omar Zirhan, and why the assassin she called Business Suit had found them so easily. Had she really been running from him, or leading him to Markaz? He was blaming Aziz's relative when the culprit could be much closer.

Until he knew where her loyalty lay, he had to keep his distance for his country's sake if not his own. All his life both interests had been as one. Now he felt them warring with each other. For the first time, the man and the monarch were as far apart as Australia and Nazaar.

Hardening his heart was almost impossible when she lay pliant and open in front of him. "No," he said harshly, letting the monarch rule the man. Even so it cost him to lever himself away. "This isn't the time or the place."

She opened huge, wounded eyes and stared at him, a rose in full bloom. "You chose both."

Sanity returned with a rush, although subduing his aching body was going to take longer. "Did I? You're not only beautiful, Simone, you're so clever it's hard to tell whether you're on the side of justice or anarchy."

Shock and hurt, real or feigned, played across her face as she struggled upright. "What? I can't believe you said that. Unless…" She trailed off, then pitched her voice low with fury. "You really haven't decided which side I'm on, have you?"

He was sorely tempted to kiss away her hurt, but that way lay madness. "I thought I knew. After the easy way Business Suit found us, I can't be sure."

Her mouth, still rosy and slightly swollen, became a thin line of outrage. "I suppose kissing a suspect is one way to get them to talk. Is that the plan, seduce me and make me spill my secrets?"

He inclined his head. "The thought crossed my mind." No point adding that talk had been the last thing he'd wanted from her until his sense of duty prevailed.

The curses she aimed at him in Arabic were normally only heard among men. Did she know what she was saying, or had someone taught her the colorful phrases as a joke? He waited until she ran out of steam, then folded his arms across his chest, the monarch back in full control. If the man lurked within, throbbing with unsatisfied desire, that was for Markaz to know and handle.

"Now it's my turn," he said. His subjects would have quailed at the deadly quiet in his voice, but Simone didn't flinch. Admiration for her gripped him until he quelled it. Such feelings were for the man, not the monarch. "You will start by telling me what you know of Omar Zirhan."

Chapter 9

Simone wasn't sure whether her outrage stemmed from the sheikh humiliating her for bursting in on the men, or his ruthless use of the attraction between them to seek information. Lost in how wonderful he made her feel, she hadn't stopped to think of a hidden agenda.

Not troubling to hide her hurt, she tightened her lips into a grim line. That they felt swollen and sensitized from his attention, she decided not to think about.

Her chin lifted. "With respect, Your Highness, there's another matter to be settled first. I won't be used for your amusement, then grilled as a suspect. First decide which I am to you, then we'll go from there."

Her anger sloughed off him. "You are either the most reckless of women, or as innocent as you claim."

"A decision only you can make, Your Highness."

"Or the police. You might not be so brave after spending a night in jail."

The words were out before she could stop them. "It would be preferable to a night in your bed."

Reaching out, he traced one finger along the line of her jaw. The touch was light, but she couldn't restrain an answering tremor. His eyes gleamed as he registered her reaction. "Are you sure?"

She willed her voice to steadiness, proud of almost achieving it. "There can be nothing between us as long as you believe I'm involved with the rebels."

"I didn't say I believed it."

"You asked me about Omar Zirhan."

"I didn't link him with the rebels. You did that."

Her stomach churned. How much more stupid could she be? He'd only asked her what she knew of Omar. Why did she have to suggest a rebel connection? If Markaz's kiss hadn't turned her mind to mush, she would have avoided the trap. Her breath rushed out. "I'm only a stupid woman, remember? What would I know of men's affairs?"

"More than you wish to tell me, evidently." Steel infused his tone. Gone was the skilled seducer whose touch reduced her to jelly. "So be it. When we reach Karama, you will be handed over to Hamal al Nawi. He will find out the truth."

She refused to give the sheikh the satisfaction of frightening her. "At last, the real face of Markaz al Nazaari," she said. "So much for the visionary working to liberate his country from the shackles of the past. When the chips are down, you don't waste time reverting to type."

"Enough," he said in a voice that could have cut glass. "You will not speak again until we reach Karama."

"Or you'll do what? Have me beaten when we get there?"

She'd finally done it, cracked his iron control. "You

are beaten," he roared. "When will you realize you are outmatched?"

Before she knew what he intended, he'd swept her into his arms again and his mouth was crushing hers. Meant as a demonstration of his power, the kiss reminded her that he was also a man who could make her body sing with desires she barely knew how to name.

She was falling and the only safety net was Markaz himself. Without his solid body to cling to, she would have toppled into the pit of her own needs. Not sure she hadn't toppled anyway, she wrapped her arms around his shoulders and answered the demands of his mouth on hers. If she couldn't tell him she was on his side, she could at least show him.

When he let her go she felt shaky. His features had softened, she saw. Was it possible she had managed to get her message across?

"You asked me to tell you what you are to me," he said, sounding as unsteady as she felt. "I only know what you could be."

"But we both know that's impossible," she said, getting in first. "You're the sheikh of sheikhs, with a country to save. I'm an independent woman who doesn't fit in here. We'd fight like cats and dogs."

He nodded. "A quaint expression, but possibly appropriate."

She stopped herself from pointing out that even cats and dogs could learn to live together. For a crazy moment she missed the spark of antagonism, carrying with it the promise of passion beyond her wildest dreams. That in itself should have served as a warning. A relationship with Markaz would be a roller coaster of the most sublime highs she'd ever known. There would also be lows of deep despair, she suspected. Who could live on a roller coaster?

"So we're agreed that what's between us can lead nowhere," she said as much to herself as to him.

"We're agreed that nothing lasting can come of what we feel," he amended. "There's no reason we can't enjoy the journey. Truce?"

She felt a tight knot start to unravel inside her. Making peace with him felt better than she wanted it to. "Truce," she agreed. "At least until I leave Nazaar." She knew it was the only thing to say, so why did her mind want to reject the words?

He reached into the bar and poured himself a glass of water, refreshing hers at the same time. Ice tinkled into the glasses and he handed her one. "Have you thought about staying? As the daughter of a Nazaari, you have the right."

She didn't tell him she'd thought about staying from the moment she stepped out of the plane at Raisa Airport. The country had woven a spell around her she hadn't expected. The stories her parents had told her about their homeland while she was growing up couldn't fully explain the sense of belonging she'd felt on arrival. Now the deeper into the country they drove, the stronger the pull became.

Her father had told her about the effect the desert region exerted on his people. She remembered the faraway look in his gaze when he'd told her about the vast ocher plains with mystical mirages shimmering in the distance. And the stark beauty of trekking by camel across waves of sand undulating like a frozen ocean.

Cold from the glass seeped into her fingers, a dose of reality. "My mother is ill. I have to go back to Australia for her."

He drank thoughtfully. "What's the matter with her?"

"After my father died she developed clinical depression and stopped taking an interest in anything. We tried having her move in with me, but she continued to get worse. Her doctor recommended a nursing home where she'd have excellent care."

"You're not happy with the decision?"

"How do you know?"

"I hear it in your voice and your posture."

Not sure she liked being read so completely, she said, "No wonder people say you preside over the majlis so effectively."

He looked gratified by the assurance. Then he shook his head. "They give me too much credit. Most of what we do in the majlis is the same as in any courtroom. Invariably, the results are unsatisfactory to one side."

"All the same, everyone I've spoken to at the palace is in awe of you."

He swirled the liquid around in his glass, staring into it. "Obviously not everyone. There is still a traitor in the royal household."

She bristled. "You have to believe that I didn't tell Business Suit where to find us today. If I was on his side, I wouldn't have given his description to the police, or alerted you to his presence at al Faransi."

After a thoughtful silence, he said, "No, you wouldn't. I should have realized that."

"An apology, Markaz?"

"As you choose."

At being given the benefit of the doubt, her spirits lifted much more than she could justify. "Couldn't he have followed us from Raisa?"

"Unlikely. Hamal's people would have noticed as we traveled."

GET FREE BOOKS and a FREE MYSTERY GIFT WHEN YOU PLAY THE...

Just scratch off the silver box with a coin. Then check below to see the gifts you get!

SLOT MACHINE GAME!

YES! I have scratched off the silver box. Please send me the 4 FREE books and mystery gift for which I qualify. I understand I am under no obligation to purchase any books, as explained on the back of this card. I am over 18 years of age.

I8CI

Mrs/Miss/Ms/Mr _____ Initials _____

BLOCK CAPITALS PLEASE

Surname _____

Address _____

_____

Postcode _____

Worth FOUR FREE BOOKS plus a BONUS Mystery Gift!

Worth FOUR FREE BOOKS!

Worth ONE FREE BOOK!

TRY AGAIN!

Visit us online at www.millsandboon.co.uk

THE READER SERVICE™
FREE BOOK OFFER
FREEPOST CN81
CROYDON
CR9 3WZ

NO STAMP
NECESSARY
IF POSTED IN
THE U.K. OR N.I.

She twisted the stem of the glass in her fingers. "He must know I've spoken to the police by now, so what does he have to gain by harming me?"

She shot him a look of frustration. "This is too cloak-and-dagger for me. I've gone over every detail of what happened from the time I met Natalie at Al-Qasr, both to the police and in my own mind. There's nothing else."

"Answers sometimes come to us when we stop trying."

"You're right," she said on a heavy sigh. "Perhaps I'll be able to think more clearly at Karama. My father said he used to do his best thinking out in the desert."

The sheikh smiled. "Ah, yes, your father was born there."

"He only left because his father married again and favored his new wife's son."

Markaz cupped his chin between thumb and forefinger. "Unusual. In our culture, firstborn sons are the most precious."

"Probably why Dad took the situation so badly. He never explained why his father preferred his stepson to his own child. Perhaps something in their different personalities."

"Do your father's people still live in Karama?" Markaz asked.

She shook her head. "The rest of my grandfather's family disapproved of the way he'd treated my father so they became estranged. I wouldn't know where to start looking for them."

"The stepson who led to your father's break with his family—is he the relative you hope to find?"

She understood his perplexity. "That's right, Yusef al Hasa. My parents never blamed him for what happened. Dad told me that Yusef was upset when Dad left home. Apparently Yusef idolized his older half brother and as soon as he could, he moved to Raisa to live with them. He must have had a winning way, because my mother was his staunchest fan."

"So Yusef managed to win over first your grandfather, and then your mother. He sounds like a silver-tongued devil."

"I gather he was. My mother hated leaving him behind although he sided with the rebels. She thought he'd been brainwashed into supporting the wrong side. She expected him to outgrow his foolishness."

Idly, Markaz lifted the hand she'd rested on the seat between them and twined his fingers through hers. The effect was instantaneous and electric, almost making her spill what was left of the water. Hastily she put the glass into the bar.

The sheikh's voice caused almost as much of a jolt. "What do you think?"

Distracted by his touch she had to force herself to link his question with her half uncle. "I think Yusef knew exactly what he was doing. Men like him are charmers. As children they use their charm unconsciously at first, but gradually learn that they can manipulate the people around them until it becomes a habit."

"That sounds like the voice of experience. With a man?"

She hadn't intended the conversation to take this turn. Cocooned in the vehicle with the tinted windows and privacy screen between them and the world, the mood easily became confessional. Too easily. "There was a man, but it's over," she said with a lightness she didn't feel.

The sheikh tightened his grip on her hand. "You are not as forgiving as your mother?"

She thought of Nick refusing to believe that she didn't

want to see him again. Like Yusef, he was also a charmer, so she understood the type well. Nick had used his charm to try to run her life, becoming annoyed at any sign of opposition.

He'd been furious with her for leaving him and threatened her. Standing up to him had been the right thing to do, she knew now. Any sign of fear on her part would have been interpreted as weakness and exploited. "I'm afraid I'm not. I was the one who ended the relationship," she said.

The sheikh frowned. "You don't want a man in your life?"

"Don't sound so amazed. A woman can exist without a man, you know." Whether or not she wanted to was another question.

Releasing her hand he turned toward the window. "You sound just like Natalie."

Yet he'd loved Natalie.

Don't even go there, Simone warned herself silently. "Hardly surprising, given that we're both independent women with minds of our own."

"Nazaari women have minds of their own, too."

She thought of Amal and smiled. What had the other woman said? In this country women were biddable and sweet until their marriage, when the man found out what he'd taken on. "I've no doubt. It's called emancipation."

"What the devil do you think I'm trying to make happen here?"

"Before you can teach others, you have to learn the lesson yourself," she said quietly. "A few seconds ago, you kissed me to prove you outmatched me."

He looked discomfited. "That was the excuse I used for doing what I wanted to do."

Nick had crowed about doing what he wanted regardless of her wishes, saying her resistance had been an act to bring him to heel. Nothing she'd said would change his mind. That was when she'd known it was over between them.

"Nobody likes being turned down," she told Markaz.

He smiled. "Ah, but you haven't turned me down yet. You simply aren't ready to face the truth. It isn't the same thing."

She struggled against anger, unhappily recognizing the truth. "Don't you get tired of being right all the time?"

Triumph gleamed in his gaze. "Then you admit I'm right about us?"

"There is no us." She wouldn't let there be.

"Yet. There is still the beauty of the desert and nights of stars such as you have never seen before. They may conspire to change your mind."

The desert was already working its magic on her. Or he was. She made herself concentrate on the scenery. They were driving across a vast plain toward a group of oases scattered along the edge of a desert known as the Lost Quarter. The occupants of a village waved as they recognized the sheikh's standard fluttering from his vehicle. Another reminder of who and what he was. And how incompatible they were.

Physical danger lurked in the beautiful surroundings, too, although the stony plain dotted with mirages and the occasional acacia tree looked anything but dangerous. Traditional nomads still wandered this region with herds of camels and sheep, their way of life almost untouched by modern life.

She saw Markaz also contemplating the landscape, then he looked back at her. "Are you ready to tell me why you sought out Omar Zirhan?"

"I suspect that Omar and Yusef are the same person," she admitted.

"Then what makes you think he's the relative you seek?"

He listened intently as she explained about the tattoo and uneven shoulder. "I know he's the same man, but he denies knowing my parents."

"Why wouldn't he acknowledge his family?"

Her eyebrows lifted. "You doubt that he's given up the rebel cause?"

"You are not the only one keeping your own counsel."

She let her breath rush out. "Can't you accept that I'm not a threat to you?"

He leaned closer, his elusive cologne teasing her. "I propose a compromise. I will agree to trust you, and you will share anything you learn from Zirhan."

Wishing her emotions wouldn't churn so furiously whenever Markaz was pleasant to her, she nodded. "All right, assuming I learn anything at all."

"You will also refrain from going off on your own," he continued in the tone of an order.

"I thought you intended to trust me?"

"It's the rebels I don't trust. The man you call Business Suit is still out there."

She felt herself blanch. "You expect him to turn up again at Karama, don't you?"

"We are probably within his sights now."

Her blood chilled. "I'll do as you say, Your Highness," she conceded.

The sheikh's dark gaze transfixed her as he lifted her hand to his mouth. His lips whispered over her fingers, making desire pool inside her. As a way to seal their bargain, it was devastatingly effective on more levels than she cared to count.

"A wise decision," he murmured.

Simone wasn't so sure.

At the royal lodge at Karama, she was given a little breathing space. For the first three days of their stay she saw no sign of Business Suit, and barely enough of Markaz himself.

Fine with her, she told herself, although small surges of resentment troubled her when she saw him from a distance looking noble in his elaborate robes, about to preside over the majlis, the traditional-style Nazaari court of justice.

At the majlis, anyone could bring a grievance to the sheikh and receive a hearing, Amal told her. Concerns could range from a request for a piece of land or a scholarship for a son or daughter, to the effect of government policies, foreign relations and employment. Discussion could be heated and intense, Amal said. People sometimes waited a week or more to see Markaz.

Except when petitioning the sheikh themselves, women weren't involved in the proceedings. They might not be segregated in a harem, but they may as well be, Simone thought. Whenever she stepped outside her room or the living rooms used by the royal women, she had to ensure her veil was in place. Not that she was often alone anyway. Amal was usually with her. And lately Bibi had taken to dogging her heels.

She couldn't blame Bibi. For a teenager separated from her boyfriend, Karama must be the height of boredom. To Simone it was the very opposite. She had never felt so much at home anywhere.

According to Amal, this lodge had been built on the ruins of an eighth-century castle destroyed by an earthquake. Little remained of the original. Now lavishly decorated pillars stood at the entrance to a central hall where Markaz held court. The vaults of the different sections opened off the core and one section was reserved for the women.

As they approached the lodge, they'd driven along a road leading to an ancient Roman reservoir half the size of a football field. This provided Karama with water and the local farmers with irrigation, Markaz had explained. Then they'd crossed a line of palm trees marking the boundary between the desolate Lost Quarter and the arc of oases surrounding the city.

Simone was fascinated by the contrast between old and new worlds. The desert might be at their door, but satellite communications and state-of-the-art computer facilities linked the lodge with the world. She was able to keep in touch with her mother, and was pleased to hear she was showing slight improvement.

She'd debated telling her mother that she was close to finding Yusef, but decided against it. If Omar turned out to be the wrong man, raising her mother's hopes could do more harm than good, particularly when the excellent care she was receiving seemed to be helping her progress.

Plus, the sheikh seemed to doubt that Omar was a hero, although everyone else thought so. Simone chafed at the restrictions keeping her from talking to the guard again.

She told herself she'd get another chance when the women went shopping at the Karama souk, the desert equivalent of a shopping mall. This souk was one of the oldest and largest in Nazaar, and Simone looked forward to seeing it. From Amal, she'd learned that Omar would be one of their escorts.

Had Markaz arranged the assignment to give Simone an opportunity to speak to Yusef? In this, her interests and the sheikh's were identical, she reminded herself when resentment struck. Markaz might be manipulating her, but she wanted to talk to Yusef, too. Until the shopping trip, she would have to bide her time.

Communicating with Drew back home and keeping up with her Internet business provided a welcome distraction. She also used the Internet to learn all she could about the rebel movement in Nazaar. Not that there was much her parents' experience hadn't taught her. They may have fled the country thirty years before, but her father had kept up to date through his newsletter.

"You spend too much time working," Amal chided after finding her at the keyboard yet again. "Wouldn't you rather watch Markaz preside over the majlis?"

Simone's fingers froze on the keyboard, her heartbeat going into automatic overdrive. "Of course, but aren't the proceedings off-limits to women?"

Amal met Simone's bitterness with a smile. "If you weren't so wrapped up in your work, you'd know that Markaz has declared the court open to all."

So he wasn't only paying lip service to reform. "When did this happen?"

"Before we left Raisa, he told me this would be the first open majlis."

"He didn't say anything on the way here." She blushed, remembering how she'd accused him of needing lessons in equality.

Amal twirled the end of her veil between thumb and forefinger. "Perhaps you had other things to discuss."

Simone closed off the computer and dragged her veil across her face to hide her heightened color. She didn't want to admit how eager she was to see the sheikh's court, but her pulse drummed in anticipation. It was the chance to see a unique aspect of Nazaari society at work, not Markaz himself fueling her excitement, she assured herself.

She kept her voice steady with an effort. "I thought we were going shopping at the souk."

"We will as soon as the morning session ends. Unless you don't want to see Markaz in action."

Simone stood up. "What are we waiting for?"

Amal's knowing smile lingered as she followed Simone out of the room.

Chapter 10

Simone hadn't expected to find such a crowd waiting for
an audience with Markaz. Guards escorted her and Amal
to where Norah and her attendant sat on cushioned
benches at the back of the vast, pillared hall. The word
majlis itself simply meant a place to sit, Simone had
learned. Most of the hundred or so people waiting to talk
to their sheikh sat on cushions on the carpeted floor. Plates
of sweets and bottles of chilled water were being handed
around. Along one back wall, a table was piled with gifts
that Amal explained were brought by the people in thanks
for the sheikh's advice.

Norah acknowledged Amal and Simone with a cool
nod. Since their arrival, the few times Simone had seen her
in the women's common rooms, the princess had been
reading or making notes, presumably for the book she
was writing. The rest of the time, Norah had kept to her

own rooms or gone walking in the grounds of the lodge, a veiled, solitary figure.

Simone focused on the majlis activity. Several local women were among the petitioners. "Why are they here?" she asked Amal.

"Probably to ask the sheikh to help them find husbands."

Simone's gaze was drawn to the raised dais where he sat flanked by his senior advisors. In immaculate white dishdasha and black embroidered surcoat, with a gold *i'qal* holding his headdress in place, he looked every inch the monarch. A fist closed around her heart.

He looked calm and solemn, giving each petitioner his full attention and the benefit of his advice. In the hubbub she couldn't hear the actual discussion, but the man in front of Markaz looked satisfied as he bowed and moved away. She saw Fayed beckon to one of the women seeking marriage.

In the brief pause while the woman approached, Markaz looked up and saw Simone, his gaze seeming to pierce the gauzy covering hiding her face. His nod of recognition was slight, but enough to make her glad that the color rushing up her neck into her face couldn't be seen.

Her skin prickled as if someone else was watching her. Not Markaz. His attention had returned to his petitioner. Simone looked around uneasily until her gaze collided with Princess Norah's. Had the woman seen the look passing between Markaz and Simone? The rigid set of the princess's body suggested she had, and was far from pleased.

You don't have to worry, I won't run off with your son, Simone wanted to assure her.

Simone was annoyed with herself for waiting like a love-struck teenager for another glance from her idol.

Amal nudged her. "Have you seen enough of our handsome sheikh at work?"

"Yes. Let's go shopping."

As they were driven to the souk, Bibi taunted her about wanting to attend the majlis, then being so eager to leave. "It's always the same old thing, squabbles over land and money, who should take care of a widow and whom a woman should marry. Dull and boring."

"Unless it's your problem being solved," Simone pointed out.

Bibi made a face. "Sheikh Markaz didn't even try to solve my problem. He took the easy way out, ordering me not to see Abdl."

Across the car Simone exchanged glances with Amal. They both knew this wasn't true. "Markaz only told you not to entertain him in your room."

Bibi's young shoulders lifted. "Same thing. Then he dragged me to the middle of nowhere for a so-called vacation. It's hardly a vacation since all he does is work."

A similar thought had occurred to Simone but she didn't voice it. Bibi's resentment was enough for both of them. "You'll enjoy yourself at the souk today," she said. After Abdl, shopping was the teenager's main preoccupation.

She wasn't alone. Most of the royal women were addicted to shopping and their closets bulged with clothing, bags and shoes all with famous designer labels. Among themselves there was a spirit of friendly competition to show off their clothes, perhaps as a reaction to wearing anonymous galabias and robes the rest of the time.

While shopping could never compete with embroidery as Simone's favorite pastime, she looked forward to seeing a real souk, having heard so much about them from her mother.

Sprawling over many blocks in the heart of the old city, Karama Souk was one of the oldest and largest in Nazaar, comprising dozens of meandering alleyways where you could buy anything from aromatic herbs to fabulous handmade carpets.

As their motorcade approached the ancient walls of the medina, Simone absorbed the sight of the narrow, winding streets crowded with shops, their wares spilling everywhere in profusion. Gold merchants, leather dealers, sellers of coffee pots and priceless carpets clamored for attention. A pharmacy like a witch doctor's den advertised cures for everything from toothache to a broken heart. Maybe she'd visit that later.

When the alleyways became too narrow and busy, they left the cars and continued on foot. Norah had surprisingly decided to join the expedition, and led their group. While Simone didn't like being under the princess's unfriendly gaze, she was pleased to notice Yusef/Omar guarding the older woman.

She intended to find an excuse to claim his attention. Getting lost wouldn't be the ideal way, she thought, knowing she'd have to keep her wits about her to avoid losing sight of the others.

A cry of "Barek" had her spinning around. "It's only a donkey delivery," Amal said, seeing her surprised reaction. "They've been delivering goods to the souk for hundreds of years."

Simone made way for the owner of the burdened animal to harass it through, then abandoned herself to the exotic sights, sounds and smells. In most stores, they were expected to drink at least one glass of sweet mint tea and spend what felt like ages in negotiations for even the smallest purchase.

"Doesn't anybody pay full price for anything in the souk?" she asked Amal, during a welcome visit to the ladies' room.

Amal smiled. "That would take the fun out of shopping."

Not sure about fun, Simone was conscious of the heat, made more stifling under her robes and veil, and of her aching feet. She restrained a sigh as they set off for another round of dress shopping. She'd bought one of the gorgeous embroidered *pashas,* a kind of two-piece galabia Amal said was worn on special occasions. For her mother she'd found a large flowing veil in French chiffon that could be worn dozens of different ways. Her purchases, along with those of the other women, would be delivered to the royal lodge later.

She'd drawn the line at the potions in the pharmacy, shuddering at the dried lizards hanging on the walls, until Amal assured her they were meant to impress the tourists, and were no longer used in modern medicine. Simone certainly hoped not. She was more enthusiastic about having her own blend of perfume made from aromatic oils and other mysterious ingredients.

She could also get used to being treated like royalty, she decided. Everywhere they went, Norah was recognized with much salaaming and deference. The rest of the royal party were also treated reverently, Simone included.

The whole experience had the flavor of a time gone by, Simone thought. Outside the stores, old men in spotless dishdashas and headdresses sat on benches whiling away the hours, others played cards or dominoes in dusty coffee shops.

Seeing Simone's feet dragging, Amal cheered her with the news that their next stop would be for lunch at an air-conditioned café in the newer part of the souk.

Newer could mean a couple of centuries old, Simone knew. While her practical side yearned for lunch and air conditioning, she probably wouldn't have the same chance to attract Yusef away from Princess Norah if the surroundings were less chaotic. She kept her eyes open for an opportunity to move closer and get his attention.

Before she could make an opportunity, she saw Bibi glance around and then duck down a side alleyway. Simone looked for Amal but she must have gone into a shop with some of the others. Although Norah was in sight, Simone didn't want her to know that Bibi was sneaking off. The teenager would get into terrible trouble if Markaz found out she'd gone off on her own.

Simone hesitated. By the time she located Amal and told her what was going on, Bibi would be out of sight. It wasn't hard to guess she intended to meet her boyfriend somewhere in the souk. What if they were found by Business Suit or some of his associates? Bibi was unaware of the danger, and probably too love struck to care. The least Simone could do was warn her, and hope she'd see reason.

Under the cover of the store displays, she kept Bibi in sight through two more alleyways until she plunged into the less frenetic Gold Souk.

As a boy, Simone's father had lived somewhere around here and had described to her the arabesque designs on the tiled floors, and the detailed murals painted at the entrance. Her grandfather had run a tiny café in the vicinity. If Ali and Sara hadn't left Nazaar, Simone would have grown up here as well. Was the café still here? Who owned it now? She wished she had time to find out.

The jammed-together stores sold all kinds of jewelry, gold coins, watches and precious stones, but Simone paid

the treasures little attention, anxious to keep her quarry in
sight. After glancing at her watch, Bibi went into a stone-
paved alley at the rear of the stores, startling a black cat
out of her path. The screech made Simone jump, too.

The only hiding place was an open door swinging to-
and-fro on creaking hinges at the back of a carpet seller's
store. She ducked behind it and watched as Bibi stopped.
Then another door opened and Abdl stepped out. If
Simone hadn't recognized him from Bibi's dreamy description, she would have worked out who he was from the
teenager's reaction.

With a cry of joy, Bibi threw herself at the young man
whose arms wrapped around her as if he never intended
to let her go. A lump rose in Simone's throat. So she was
right, this was an assignation between the young lovers.

She felt her eyes film. Bibi would get herself into real
trouble if she thought she could defy Markaz's orders
again. Simone had started to move forward to warn the
lovers, but they disappeared around a corner. Then
someone grabbed her from behind. She was pulled through
the doorway, her cry of alarm cut off by the clang of the
metal door slamming shut. Had Bibi and Abdl heard her
or were they too preoccupied with each other?

Hampered by her clothes, she swung around, but the
man who grabbed her was smiling and salaaming. He
looked to be about sixty, almost as wide as he was tall, his
mustache and hair peppered with gray. "Forgive the insen-
sitive treatment, Your Highness, but you are in a dangerous
place. Lately ladies wandering out of the main thorough-
fares have been set upon, and their valuables stolen."

She could hardly believe her ears. "You're rescuing me?"

"Indeed, Your Highness. I am Nayan al Kitab. Usually
I keep the back door locked and bolted, but I had closed

up for the lunch break, and was about to step out when I saw you there. I couldn't live with myself if anything happened to you outside my establishment."

Nayan thought she was a member of the royal family. Her veil fluttered as she released a breath of relief. "I'm perfectly all right," she assured him. "I was following a companion. We're supposed to meet our escort not far from here."

The carpet seller frowned. "There are some dwellings along the next street facing the souk. If you intended to go there, you have taken a wrong turn. A back alley is not an appropriate place for a young lady to meet anyone, Your Highness."

Simone seethed inwardly. What right had this man to interfere in her activities for her own protection, just because he was male? He was probably one of those old-fashioned men who thought society would crumble if women were allowed to think for themselves. But arguing would only prolong the encounter, so she adopted a pose of feminine submission. "You're quite right. I'll be more careful in the future," she said, curbing her anger.

He saw it anyway, but misunderstood. "You are distraught. Come, sit in my humble store. I'll have mint tea brought for you while you regain your composure."

Nayan ushered Simone into an Aladdin's cave of carpets, and urged her to make herself comfortable on a cushioned banquette. Her heart rate was slowly returning to normal. Her head had realized she was safe, but her body was still catching up.

Rubbing her clammy hands against her galabia, she cursed herself. Following Bibi had been foolhardy. So many things could have gone wrong. What would she have done if Business Suit had grabbed her, instead of an interfering but well-meaning merchant? Assuming he was well-meaning.

Rattled by the thought, she got up and tried the front door. Locked. Many of the shops in the souk closed for lunch. Breaking out seemed a bit extreme without evidence of a real threat, so she returned to the banquette and sat down, but not before placing one of the brass ornaments within grabbing distance to use as a weapon if needed.

From the back of the shop and she heard the murmur of voices. She tensed as the door to the back of the shop opened, but it was only the carpet seller returning. A few seconds later, a young boy, his son she presumed, appeared with a brass teapot and tiny cups.

As soon as he'd served the tea, the son disappeared and she guessed Nayan had sent the boy to alert the royal party. She investigated the huge variety of carpets, but they offered her no way out.

She was cradling a second, equally unwelcome cup of tea when a hammering on the door jolted her host. Nayan sprang up and opened the door. Her heart sank when she saw Fayed standing there, with no sign of Yusef. Fayed hadn't been with them during the morning. What was he doing here now?

"Come, Sima," he ordered without preamble.

She got to her feet. "Good to see you again too, Fayed."

Her sarcasm was wasted on the giant. "Sheikh Markaz ordered me to bring you to him at once."

"How did he know where to find me?"

"Your absence caused enough concern for it to be reported to His Highness."

She hadn't anticipated that. "I can take care of myself."

Fayed shot her a withering look. "So I see."

"I was in good hands with Nayan. He sent his son to tell Princess Norah where I am."

The bodyguard barely glanced at the other man. "You should not have wandered away from the others."

Tempted to stand up for her right to go where she pleased, she remembered barely in time who she was supposed to be and why. This must be how Bibi felt at being ordered not to see her young lover, she thought. Under Fayed's stern gaze, Simone felt as if she were Bibi's age.

Her mood didn't improve when Fayed hustled her out of Nayan's shop as if she'd caused more trouble than she was worth. "You could at least have thanked the man for his kindness," she snapped.

Fayed's stony gaze didn't soften. "We must not keep Sheikh Markaz waiting."

Oh, she wouldn't keep him waiting, she resolved. As soon as they were alone, she'd tell Markaz exactly what she thought of being treated so peremptorily. She might be hiding in his harem but that didn't mean she'd abandoned her rights.

She had expected to be taken to Princess Norah and the other women. Instead, Fayed led her to a car waiting outside the souk. "Won't the others wonder where I went?" she asked when they were heading along the road leading to the lodge. The bodyguard had taken his usual seat up front beside the driver, but had left the privacy screen open as if fearing she'd jump out at the first opportunity.

When Fayed didn't answer, she sat back fuming. If Markaz had ordered Fayed to bring him her head on a platter, would he have done that, too? She decided she didn't want to know. Her hope that Yusef would be sent to escort her back to the group had come to nothing. Now she had no idea when she would be able to talk with the guard on his own.

By the time they reached the lodge, her temper was at flashpoint. "I'm dusty and disheveled. I can't possibly appear before the sheikh in this condition," she snapped when Fayed tried to urge her in the direction of the sheikh's courtroom.

The giant didn't argue. He merely hefted her over his shoulder and carried her through the halls, ignoring her futile squirming and angry protests. A few minutes later, he dumped her outside the courtroom as if she were the day's laundry. "His Highness is waiting for you," he rumbled.

Restoring her clothes and her dignity as much as possible, she lifted her head. "When I tell Markaz about this, he'll probably have you flogged."

The last thing she heard as the huge double doors closed behind her was the low rumble of the giant's laughter.

Markaz wasn't laughing, she saw as she stalked to the low dais where he'd held court. His expression was thunderous, making her quail inwardly although she kept her head high. Her face was hot from being carried over Fayed's shoulder, not from confronting the sheikh, she assured herself.

The hall was empty now, her footsteps echoing on the marble floor. Good. What she intended to say to Markaz was probably better not said in front of others.

"I must protest Fayed's high-handed treatment," she said when she was close enough to speak normally, although she was slightly amazed that she still could.

Markaz held up a hand. "Stop there."

He'd indicated the place where applicants to the majlis stood to state their concerns. Surely he didn't see her in that role? Defiantly she took a few steps closer. "With respect, I'm not one of your courtiers. That…that body-guard of yours actually threw me over his shoulder and dropped me outside your door."

"He was acting on my instructions."

"I can't believe you told him to treat me like a piece of lost property."

Markaz stood up, looming over her although the dais wasn't high. "In my kingdom, you are property."

"I was right then. Despite paying lip service to reform, you aren't in a hurry to change the law because it would limit your right to be a petty tyrant when it suits you."

With a swirl of robes he stepped down from the dais and came to within a heartbeat of her. "Is that how you see me, as a petty tyrant?"

She drew herself up, her veil fluttering with the sudden shallowing of her breathing. "If the cap fits."

Anger warred with something else she couldn't identify on his features. "You are the most impossible female I've ever had to deal with."

"Then don't deal with me. Treat me as a normal human being with a mind of my own."

Some of his anger dissipated visibly, although his hands remained clenched at his sides, she saw. "I never doubted that you have a mind of your own." Then he had to spoil things. "It's common sense you seem to lack."

"Because I'm female?" she said with a defiance she was far from feeling. His closeness was eroding her anger, and what remained made her feel terrifyingly vulnerable.

"Because you don't seem to realize the risk you took by slipping away from the group." Unclenching a hand, he lifted it to her face and released her veil. The gauze flut-tered to one side.

Her feeling of vulnerability increased, tempting her to

replace the veil. Without it she felt as if he could see into her soul. "You were worried about me?"

"I thought you'd been kidnapped."

Telling herself not to read more than concern in his expression, she nodded. "So did I when the carpet seller pulled me into his shop. But he was only making sure no harm came to me."

"What were you doing in that area in the first place?"

Simone lowered her gaze. "The souk is confusing. It's easy to lose your way." Not exactly a lie, and she avoided betraying Bibi and Abdl.

The sheikh's hand came under her chin and he lifted her head so she couldn't avoid his searching look. "There is so much between us, and still you will not tell me the truth."

Chapter 11

The floor under her feet felt rocky suddenly. She addressed the only part of his assertion she could. "There's nothing between us." Nothing she would allow, anyway.

"Another lie, Simone?"

"A necessity."

She hadn't meant to be so frank, although her mind resonated with the need. She couldn't let herself feel what she felt when she was around him, but neither did she know how to stop. His presence, his male scent, even his anger wove a web around her that threatened to tighten until she couldn't think straight. Yet she must.

Being in control of her life wasn't just important to her, it was essential. She'd seen the consequence of her parents being driven out of their country and having to start over in a strange land. She had promised herself nothing like that would ever happen to her. Her life would be planned, orderly, and she would be in the driving seat no matter what.

Nothing in her careful planning had anticipated Markaz.

If she gave in to his attraction, she would have to consider following her parents' path and pulling her life out by the roots, transplanting herself to a land as foreign to her as Australia had been to Sara and Ali. There could be no question of Markaz leaving Nazaar. He *was* Nazaar.

As if unable to stop himself, he let his knuckles trail down her cheek. "There are many kinds of necessity."

She gestured around them, aware that her control hung by a thread. Somehow she had to fix that before she said or did something completely stupid. Like let his touch reduce her to jelly. She locked her knees to steady herself. "Your position being the biggest one." Also the biggest obstacle between them.

He heard what she hadn't said. "I'm not always on duty."

"But you're always on call. I watched you presiding over the majlis this morning. You had solutions for everybody's problems."

"Except one."

Her curiosity flared. "Which one?"

"What I should do about you. You drive me mad with wanting you, yet you have no respect for my authority."

"I do respect your authority," she argued.

He shook his head. "You see? You cannot resist challenging me at every turn."

She brushed aside the veil dangling down one side of her face. "Am I supposed to accept whatever you say because you're the sheikh?"

His laughter warmed her. "There's no chance you'll go

that far. I would settle for you keeping your word. You promised you would not go off alone until the rebel threat is resolved."

"Getting lost isn't the same as breaking a promise."

His fingers grasped her chin, forcing her to face him. "Dissembling again? Why can't you admit you were helping Bibi to keep an assignation with Abdl?"

"I wasn't helping them." Too late she realized she'd been maneuvered into admitting she knew about the teenagers' meeting. "You know about that?"

He nodded. "So you may as well tell me everything."

"I went after her to make sure she was all right."

"Were you worried she or Abdl might be the traitor?"

Simone pulled away from him. "I'm convinced they're not."

"What makes you so sure?"

"If you'd seen them, you'd know the only thing driving them is love."

He crossed his arms. "As it happens, I agree with you. They are only foolish children. And proof of the dangerously stupid things an overrated emotion makes people do," he growled.

Was he talking about the teenagers or himself? She refused to think she had such an effect on Markaz, unless the responses tearing through her weren't all on her side. She pushed the possibility away. "Don't Nazaari poets say that to die in love is martyrdom?"

"They also say love is a journey of the soul toward paradise," he answered. "In my experience, a journey with too many hazards along the way."

"But you don't deny the outcome?"

His gaze fastened on her. "I agree there are sublime moments."

Her emotions jolted as she filled in the gaps. The journey would be in his bed with paradise the likely destination. She felt heat surge into her face and almost pulled the veil back into place as a gesture of self-protection.

Instead, she resorted to words. "Why are we talking about love when the real issue between us is trust?"

"I thought we were talking about sex."

Instead of shocking her, his bluntness fueled another jagged surge of desire. She tamped it down, not sure how successfully. "Neither is appropriate right now."

"Do you always behave appropriately?"

If she had, Fayed wouldn't have dragged her in here, she thought. "How did you know that Bibi was meeting Abdl?" she asked, attempting to change the subject.

Markaz went to a side table and poured water into a glass from a carafe. When he offered her some, she shook her head. Her throat was dry and her head pounded, but water wasn't the answer. What *would* make her feel better didn't bear thinking about.

He sipped the water. "They told me themselves. They heard you scream when you were pulled through the door. When Abdl couldn't find you, he contacted Hamal who reported to me."

"Then it's my fault they were discovered."

His expression hardened. "It's their own fault. But their courage in helping you will be rewarded. I have arranged an engagement between them. A long engagement."

Pleased for the youngsters who had risked so much on her behalf, she asked, "Does that mean they can see each other openly?"

"They will be under their parents' supervision. Bibi is returning home and Abdl is going to work for her father in his business until they're old enough to marry."

Simone flung her arms around his shoulders, almost spilling the water. "That's wonderful. I'm so happy for them." Then her eyes narrowed. "You didn't arrange all that today."

He put the endangered glass down and grasped her arms, stopping her from pulling away. His dark gaze fastened on her. "I set the wheels in motion before we left Raisa. Despite what you evidently think, I do have a heart."

Her breath tangled. "I know."

"Then you know it's racing right now."

She could feel the beat. Her own was keeping time. Fool, she told herself. Keeping her distance made more sense than throwing herself at him. Her joy on Bibi and Abdl's behalf had only provided an excuse. She had wanted to be exactly where she was. What to do next was the problem.

When she tried to step back, he held her in place. "I have yet to impose a penalty for breaking your word."

He was imposing one now, holding her close enough for his breath to whisper over her cheeks, his mouth within kissing distance. Sweet torture indeed. "What do you have in mind?" she asked, her voice barely functioning.

"What would you suggest?"

Her thoughts whirled and she said the first thing springing to mind. "Confine me to my room?"

"I'd rather confine you to mine."

"Because of the danger I'm in from the rebels?" Great. Now she was stammering like a fool.

His dark eyes gleamed. "Because of the danger you're in from me."

"I don't understand." But she was all too sure she did.

"From the moment I saw you at Al-Qasr, I felt a connection between us. The longer we're together, the stronger the feeling becomes. Soon, I won't be able to let you go at all."

"Then let me go now, while you still can. It's what I want, too." Would he recognize another lie?

He shook his head. "We passed the point when I could willingly let you go the first time I kissed you. I knew then that you were becoming important to me."

Recognition dawned. "You don't like it any more than I do."

He closed his eyes and opened them again. She almost recoiled from the anguish she read in their depths. "No, I don't." He sounded as if the admission were being dragged out of him. "One foreign wife who hated living here was enough. My next wife must love my country as I do, and provide the heirs to ensure future stability."

She couldn't hide her own hurt. "You see, you do have the solution."

His hands flew to her arms and he pulled her closer. "This pleases you?"

So close to him, feeling his body heat radiating through her, she could give only one response. "No."

"It's the sane, logical course of action. But around you I feel neither sane nor logical."

She could say the same for herself. "What are we going to do?"

"Right now, there is only one thing I want to do."

His mouth found hers in a hot, hungry kiss that sent her senses reeling. The power of his passion hammered through her, and she arched against him. All thought of punishment fled. This was seduction, pure and simple.

His hands stroked her back, slid lower to cup her bottom and pull her against him. Instantly she became aware of his arousal and her own soared.

With an effort she forced her eyes open and the fog in her mind to recede. "This isn't…we can't…"

His lips teased hers. "We can do anything we want."

She felt herself chill. "Perhaps you can, because of who you are. It isn't so simple for me."

A few strands of hair had escaped her scarf and he brushed them out of her eyes. "This isn't about my rights as the sheikh, only as a man."

"The man didn't have me carried through the corridors and dumped at his feet."

"But he wanted to."

Markaz saw the shock freeze her into place. That made two of them, he thought. He hadn't intended to voice the admission, but he couldn't—wouldn't—deny the truth. Hearing she'd been taken had so enraged him that he'd ordered everyone out of his sight while he regained control. Only years of royal discipline had stopped him from going after her himself. He'd told Fayed to bring her to him the instant they returned because Markaz had to see for himself that she was all right. As usual, Fayed had interpreted the order in his own way.

The sheikh didn't need any of this. Not the passion, the caring or the involvement that was wrong for himself and his country. But the man did. He needed to kiss Simone as desperately as a wanderer in the desert needs water to survive.

He lifted her hand to his mouth and kissed her fingers, feeling the jolt as she tried to pull away. "I can't change what I am, but I am also more than my title."

"We're wrong for each other in too many ways to list," she said.

"Then let me ask you this. Do you find me unattractive?"

Her expression betrayed her even before she said, "No."

"Are you a virgin?"

"N-no."

"Do you find lovemaking unpleasant?"

A longer hesitation before he felt her fingers tense in his. Then she said, "No."

"Do you require the promise of marriage before making love?"

She twisted in his grasp. "Obviously not, or I'd be married by now."

He let her create a heartbeat of space between them, but retained hold of her hand. Easy enough to reel her in when she was ready. "I feel exactly the same way. So what objections remain?"

Control, she thought. Control was the issue. His interrogation only added to her panic that he could take over her life as easily as he commanded her physical responses. Already his questions had inflamed needs she couldn't push away.

She did find him attractive. More than attractive. Around him, she could hardly think of anything else. Away from him, she was consumed with wondering where he was and what he was doing.

She enjoyed lovemaking with the right man. But how could she know if Markaz was the right man? By making love with him. A dilemma indeed.

"Can't you simply take no for an answer?" she snapped, as annoyed with herself as with him.

He lifted their joined hands. "Not when your trembling tells me you want to say yes."

Her hand wasn't the only part of her quaking. She was glad he didn't know the full extent of his effect on her. "Then read my lips. I don't want…"

Before she could complete the sentence, his mouth crushed hers. As he deepened the kiss, the last of her resistance vanished. He felt the change when she stopped trying to free her hand and curled her fingers tighter around his.

He lifted his head, his eyes flaming. "You were going to tell me something."

She shook her head, her expression dazed. "I was, but it's gone now."

He trailed kisses along the line of her jaw, her shivers of pleasure echoing his own tremors as she arched against him. "Good. For now I want you to think only of me."

The gaze she directed at him was troubled. "And later?"

"There is no later, only now."

"Only now," she repeated. If only it were true. "Such a wonderful fantasy."

Through the silk of her galabia he molded her breast, thrilling to her softness contrasting with the pebbled nipple he felt pressing against his palm. "The fantasy has barely begun, my beautiful Sima."

She could do this. Live the fantasy. Revel in the moment. The days of women needing a promise of forever were long gone. Whether the hope of a happy ever after lingered at the back of her mind was for her alone to know and deal with.

"Yes," she said on a huge outpouring of breath. The rightness of the one word crashed through her. She wanted him here, now, no more dissembling. While he was still the man and not the sheikh of sheikhs.

He'd said there was no later, but there would be. He would change back into the sheikh, and she into an independent Western woman. But that was no reason not to enjoy this time together. Choosing to surrender control wasn't the same as having it taken from her. A fantasy, he called it. Surely every woman was entitled to one?

She was quivering with anticipation as he took her hand and walked her toward a billowing curtain at the back of the dais. Pushing through the folds, he brought her into a room the size of a suburban bedroom back home. The walls and low ceiling were rough-textured plaster, painted white with a single high window letting sunlight slant through. Other than the inevitable Persian carpets layered over the marble floor, there was little in the way of furnishings. Only a table containing a carafe, a glass, a tray of refreshments and, on the far wall, a narrow couchette banked with cushions.

She could barely mask her disappointment. This was his idea of a fantasy setting? Desire for him throbbed through her like a living thing. She could no more have gone away unfulfilled than she could have flown under her own power. But surely a more romantic backdrop wasn't expecting too much?

Perhaps it was better this way, she thought. Keep things purely physical so she didn't lose sight of their true relationship. But as she moved toward the couchette, he tugged on her hand. "During the majlis, this is my retreat when I need to consult advisors or consider a decision."

She scanned the chamber, but saw no other doors. "That only leaves the floor."

The carpets were lovely and probably worth a fortune, but not in the least inviting for what he had in mind. She began to have second and third thoughts. "Maybe this isn't a good idea after all."

"Wait."

Too aroused and curious, she did as bidden. He went to what looked like a blank wall, tapped a point a few feet up from the floor and the same distance from the corner, and turned to her with an expression of almost boyish delight. "Watch."

She took the hand he held out, and gasped as a crack and then a hidden door opened in the wall. Feeling like Alice stepping through the looking glass, she walked through with him, hearing the door grate closed behind them. Turning, she saw that the door had disappeared again. Knowing the secret, she could probably find it if she had to, but wouldn't count on doing so easily.

Whatever she had expected, it wasn't the chamber meeting her astonished gaze. Like something out of an *Arabian Nights* tale, the room was tented with filmy white fabric, with thick carpets underfoot and painted walls glowing like mother-of-pearl under concealed lighting. Low cabinets and a bar were along one wall. In the center, a carpeted platform supported a deep mattress piled with jewel-colored coverings and voluminous pillows. Through an archway she glimpsed an en suite bathroom. Cool air whispered against her heated skin from some hidden source.

If ever a room was made for romance, this was the place. Utterly decadent, totally private. The pounding sensation inside her notched higher.

"What is this place?" she asked, automatically lowering her voice although she was sure no one could possibly overhear.

He confirmed it when he said, "There's no need to whisper. This is known as the royal chamber. In earlier times, the sheikh and his family could hide out here if the lodge was attacked by marauders from the desert."

"Was the chamber ever used for that purpose?"

"Many times. It was less lavishly furnished then, and provisioned for a siege."

She turned to him, struggling against jealousy of the women he must surely have brought here before her. "Whose idea was it to equip it as a bedroom?"

His mouth turned up slightly, as if he sensed her suspicion. "Not mine, if that's what you're asking. It was my mother's idea."

Simone felt her jaw slacken. Trying to imagine the cold, unapproachable Norah creating such a boudoir was almost beyond her.

"She loved my father very much," Markaz said quietly.

Looking at the lovely, romantic furnishings, Simone felt a lump clog her throat. "So I see."

"Every sheikh passes on the secret of this room to his sons," Markaz explained. "When my turn came, my father told me it had been used just once in his marriage, the night I was conceived."

The lump grew. "What about your older brother?"

"My father spoke only of me."

Did Markaz wonder, as she did, at the significance of this? So much love and passion infused the chamber, she could feel it. Or was her own passion answering the siren call of the surroundings?

"You are the first woman I've brought to this room," he added.

Her knees went weak and she stumbled.

Instantly Markaz was there, sweeping her into his arms, setting off a fresh explosion of need inside her. She wrapped her arms around his neck, sensations tearing through her like wildfire. His muscular chest felt like a rock wall, making her ache to tear away the robes and connect with him skin to skin, flesh joining with flesh.

"Does anyone else know of this chamber?" she asked.

"Only my most trusted personal servant and Fayed and

Hamal for security reasons. They can reach me here in a dire emergency."

The implication was clear. They would not be disturbed for anything less than a threat to national security.

When he placed her on the bed, she released him with a reluctance he noticed. "It's only for a moment, my Sima," he said. "I have no intention of leaving you for long."

He meant for the duration of the fantasy, she knew, but chased the thought away. He didn't want to love her or need her any more than she wanted to love him. No promises had been made, except the implied one of shared pleasure. The very thought made her womb clench, and she fisted the jeweled coverlet in shaking hands. No man had gifted her with unconditional pleasure before. All she had to do was accept his gift in the spirit he offered it, with no thought of tomorrow.

"You're thinking too much," he said, his tone faintly accusing. He stood looking down at her, a small, mosaic-covered box in his hands. "For as long as we remain here, I want you thinking only of me."

Her throat dried. "I *was* thinking of you."

Placing the box on a side table, he sat on the platform and raised her hand to his mouth, his lips whispering over her fingertips. "Seeing you waiting for me, how can I think of anything else?"

He raised her so he could slip the galabia off over her head. The modern lace bra she wore underneath seemed incongruous in this setting, but she heard his breath catch at the sight of her breasts cupped in white lace. The bra fastened at the front and he unhooked it so she spilled into his hands. "Your beauty takes my breath away," he said, bending over her.

The suckling sensation was almost too much. She gave up trying to keep her mind clear, and let her head drop back. When he trailed kisses down her body, every nerve short-circuited in unison and she bucked under his hands. She hardly felt him slide the silk *sirwall* down her legs, leaving her in the lace panties matching her discarded bra.

A hint of breeze brushed over her as he stood up. First he removed the *i'qal* and headdress, setting them aside. Then he stripped off his robes, letting them pool on the floor. She could hardly take her eyes off his magnificence. His chest muscles were as sculpted as she'd suspected, veeing to narrow hips and strong legs. Seeing him naked for the first time, she knew he truly deserved the title, sheikh of sheikhs.

She reached for his hands to pull him down beside her. And met resistance. "In good time, my beauty."

"If you're trying to make me beg, you're about to get your wish."

He smiled. "So soon? We've barely begun."

She was on fire and this was just the beginning? Anxiety fluttered in her chest at the reminder of how completely she had placed herself in his hands. She couldn't even count on finding the way out of this room on her own.

This was a fantasy, an interlude, she reminded herself to counter the uncertainty. Nothing would happen without her consent, and afterward she would be back in control of her life, the way she wanted to be.

Didn't she?

His fingers played inside the lace edge of her panties, making her squirm. "The meeting of souls shouldn't be rushed."

Her stomach muscles contracted at his touch. She pulled in air that didn't reach the bottom of her lungs. "I've never heard lovemaking described as a meeting of souls before."

"You've never been with me before."

What could have sounded like arrogance, Markaz turned into a promise. She dragged her fingers through her hair, realizing belatedly that the move made her breasts more prominent. Resisting the temptation to cover them she said, "Not everybody is as sure of themselves as you."

He traced circles around her sensitized nipples, earning a sharply indrawn breath. "What are you unsure about, my beautiful Sima?"

"Being here. Doing this." *Surrendering,* she added silently.

"We can stop anytime you want. Do you?"

"No."

"Then tell me you want me."

He wasn't making this easy. She didn't want to want him, but her body—her soul?—had other ideas. "I want you to make love to me," she said.

"That isn't what I asked."

She bolted upright against the pillows, confused by his comment. "Is there a difference?"

"A difference as vast as the sands of the Lost Quarter. Wanting me to make love to you is no more than a mare wants from a stallion. Wanting *me* means your soul calling to mine, giving you no peace until we become one."

The distinction was the very reason for her ambivalence. Wanting him felt far safer than wanting to be one with him. She'd thought he would settle for the same deal. Was she being unfair expecting him to? "I didn't mean to insult you."

"It's yourself you insult. You don't know how hard I've resisted bringing you to this room. Or what it means now that I have."

She moved her head from side to side. "I thought we could enjoy a romantic interlude, then go our separate ways."

"With us, there can be no separate ways. You sense the link between us as strongly as I do." He rose to one knee on the platform. "What you choose to do about it is up to you. If you tell me truthfully that you don't want me, I'll open the secret door and let you go."

She swallowed hard. "But the link will still be there?"

"Always."

The sensible move would be to let him open the door. She'd be back in control. Running her own life. Alone. Never knowing if the yearning she felt to the depths of her being was caused by his soul link, or simply by unfulfilled desire.

She had to know.

Chapter 12

Drawing her legs up, she clasped her arms around them, trying to sort her body's demands from her mind's with little success. "You accused me of thinking too much. Isn't this the same thing?" Trembling with arousal, the last thing she wanted was to talk.

He wasn't done yet. "I want you to think about me. Not the act of fulfillment, but the man giving you pleasure."

How could she not? She rubbed a finger along a furrow between her eyes. "Easy for you to say. You're the one in control."

She saw understanding dawn. "Ah, that is what troubles you?"

"Yes." Her answer was a whisper of torment.

He stroked his palm down the length of her thigh, eliciting a soft moan. "The only reason we struggle to maintain control is fear. You have nothing to fear from me, my beauty."

Offering his hand, he helped her off the bed and took her to the wall they'd come through. Was he going to send her away after all? But he placed her hand against the cool stone until she felt the texture of a mechanism. She smiled. "I can feel the lock."

"Good. By pressing it, you can open the door any time."

He understood. Not everything, but enough for relief to flood her. "This—fear—started with my father. He was so afraid of anything happening to my mother or me that he controlled every aspect of our lives. After he died, I got involved with someone who tried to do the same. But he was only living up to my expectation that a man would run my life."

Markaz cupped her face in two hands. "So you left him and came to Nazaar, where men have been running women's lives for centuries."

She felt her eyes mist. "Crazy, isn't it?"

"Or a way of facing your deepest fear. That takes courage."

Unable to look away, she lowered her lashes. "I didn't mean to get into this. We came here for sex."

"We came here to make love," he said, his kisses smoothing out her frown. "Understanding you enables me to please you without scaring you. I'll ask you again. Do you want me?"

At the soft touch of his mouth, her heart hammered against her ribs. "Yes. I want you, Markaz."

"Then show me."

She knew what he was doing. After her admission that men had done the running of her life until now, Markaz was letting her set the pace. After a moment of uncertainty, she took his hand and led him back to the bed. "Lie down."

"All right."

He stretched out full length, his head filling the dent she'd left in the pillow. She allowed herself a long perusal of his beautiful body, then reached out. When she stroked his flank his breath caught, but he stayed quiet. Waiting. At least most of him did.

The part that didn't had her eyes widening. "Is this torture for you?"

His eyes glittered. "In the most exquisite way. Fortunately, Nazaari men are taught agility and control as part of our education."

Starting to enjoy herself, she knelt on the platform and brushed her hands over his chest, playing her fingers down his ribs like a pianist. How lean and hard he was. She bent and kissed him, letting her tongue tickle the corners of his mouth. A low groan edged around her lips. His or hers, she wasn't entirely sure.

When she lifted her head, she saw his hands fisting the bedcovers. He'd bent one leg and his breathing was shallow, as if he hovered on the brink.

She gulped. "I think I've had enough of being in charge for now."

He opened his arms. "We can take turns."

Now it was his turn. She'd already pushed his self-control to the limit. When she lay down beside him, he had to fight the urge to lose himself in her now. He forced himself to wait. To heighten her pleasure before claiming his own.

Rolling onto his side, he slowly traced kisses down the cleft between her beautiful breasts, feeling her tremble. He allowed himself to taste the honeyed tips, to slide his teeth around the nubs and tease them with his tongue.

"Markaz." Part cry, part plea.

He rested his head against her, breathing lightly. When he was sure he had himself under control, he began to outline her body in kisses, his mouth exploring every inch of her in luxurious detail.

This was so new, so amazing. She could barely think for the sensations layering themselves one upon another, giving her no time to recoup in between. All she could do was feel.

Her thoughts swirled. Her fingers tangled in his hair without conscious intent, and she pressed back against the jeweled nest, expecting it to swallow her up at any second. When it did, she screamed her torment and delight, going rigid then boneless as wave after wave of ecstasy shook her.

He lifted his head, his eyes bright. "You're amazing."

"No, you are. I haven't…I've never…"

His finger pressed against her lips. "I told you we've barely begun."

Floating on a cloud, she felt unfocused, as if she'd shattered into pieces. He'd already given her so much. How could there be more?

Unbelievably, there was.

Through heavy-lidded eyes she watched as he levered himself up and reached for the mosaic box on the bedside. Opening it, he took out a bulblet of iridescent liquid. He set the box aside. "These are love pearls, to heighten one's pleasure."

Watching him tip a few drops of the liquid into his hand, she felt dizzy with anticipation. Her voice felt unsteady as she started to ask, "Then how do you…oh."

He swooped over her and his touch became even more intimate, massaging and sensitizing her almost beyond belief as the contents of the pearl perfumed the air with the heady fragrance of exotic herbs. His fingers sliding over her skin as he anointed her threatened to drive her to melting point.

She couldn't stop reaction cascading across her face, his enjoyment mirroring hers. "The pearls contain rare Arabian aromatics designed to enhance a woman's readiness."

She felt as if she was raging out of control. "What do you get?" she managed to ask.

He let his gaze linger on her before answering. "Isn't it obvious? You."

His breathing turned ragged. He rolled until he lay across her, propped up on his arms. "You have the most amazing effect on me, my Sima."

With her hand trapped between them, she felt his heart hammering and her own keeping time. "What happened to agility and control?"

"The techniques are not foolproof, and can be overpowered if the hunger is strong enough."

"And is it?"

He traced a line around her mouth, his hard body pressing her back against the cushions. "Need you ask?"

"No." The answer was in the urgent way he pressed against her, his tongue circling her breasts until she was so swamped by sensation she couldn't draw a whole breath.

If she spun much further out of control, she would shatter into bits. "Now, Markaz," she urged.

He kissed her parted lips. "Very soon, my lovely." He rolled away, opened the mosaic box and took out a condom this time.

She felt hot and aching. "That coffer is full of magic."

He shook his head. "The magic is in us. In you, my Sima. You were made for this."

"Only because of you." No other man had ever made her feel so wanton, so desirable. Out of control, but not afraid because she had chosen this. Chosen him. In a fever of anticipation, she watched as he sheathed himself. Supporting himself on his arms, he moved over her, but held himself away a little, teasing her with gentle nudges until her excitement was almost explosive. She threaded her fingers through his hair, pulling his head down and feasting on his sensuous mouth.

When she stopped to gulp in air, he looked fully into her open eyes. Did he see the soul-deep connection she could feel linking them? Slowly, deeply, inexorably, he filled her, driving the breath out of her and replacing it with his potent maleness. His taste infused her as his movements became deeper, harder, more powerful than anything in her experience. Her nails dug into his shoulders as she absorbed sensation after sensation, taking all he offered and more, giving more than she'd thought she could possibly give.

Her precious control wavered, teetered then blew apart in a sudden surge of feeling sweeping her upward, higher and higher. She gloried in the way his body molded to hers as he held her. His mouth was hot and hungry on her lips. She was flying, shooting for the moon, and fear was a speck left behind on the ground.

When he threw back his head and howled her name, she felt herself plummet over the edge into the void.

The room took a long time to stop spinning. Weakly, but feeling like a cat with cream on its whiskers, she stretched, trying not to disturb Markaz who lay with his head pillowed against her breast. He awoke and rolled onto his back, pulling her with him into the curve of his arm. "Being out of control isn't so bad, is it?" he asked, sounding as sated as she felt.

"I could get used it. With a little more practice."

His mouth curved. "An invitation, my Sima?"

She sighed. More like wishful thinking. "You make my name sound so poetic."

"This is a time for poetry. And for other things."

Thinking of the other things, she felt her face heat. "Won't someone be missing you by now?"

"The majlis is over for the time being. Normally I'd be busy with paperwork at this hour."

"Instead of with me."

He caressed her breast lightly, speeding her pulse. "I know where I prefer to be."

"Oh, Markaz, I have no herbal pearls, no training in the bedroom arts."

He kissed each breast in turn, laving her nipples with his tongue until she writhed in his hold. "Don't discount the value of instinct."

Hers was telling her she wanted him again, and she surprised herself by saying so.

"Already?" he asked, sounding pleased.

She could see his strength returning. "Unless it's too much for you."

He rolled over, finding her mouth. "We'll soon see about that."

Whoever said too much of a good thing was never enough had the right idea, she decided. Aching, but feeling more alive than she had in years, she lay in the crook of Markaz's arm, listening to his even breathing. His broad chest rose and fell rhythmically. There was a faint, crescent-shaped scar under his ribs. Idly she traced over it with her finger.

Soon duty would call him away. She didn't want to think about that. Or about leaving Nazaar when the time came.

So she thought about how far she had come. Not only in distance from her birthplace, but in her own growth. Markaz was right, she sensed. Her need to be in control of her life had been driven by fear. Knowing she could let go without the world coming to an end was a big step.

It wouldn't last, but she could enjoy the feeling for now. Time enough to worry about the real world when they were forced to rejoin it.

"You're thinking again," Markaz said, stirring. He laced his fingers through hers. "Are you curious about the scar?"

She was curious about everything to do with him. "Tell me you got it in a sword fight, or an altercation with desert raiders."

"Nothing so romantic. I tried to drive my father's favorite car before I could see over the steering wheel. I crashed it in the palace grounds at Raisa."

"Not very princely behavior."

"No, but as the younger son, I wasn't being groomed for the throne so I was permitted more freedom than my brother, Esan. I thought I could do anything I wanted."

She could imagine him as a headstrong child, full of boyish exuberance. Traces of those qualities lingered in the man, although under much tighter control nowadays. "What else did you get up to?"

"When I was nine, I tried to sell copies of my father's signature to the boys at my school."

"How enterprising."

His hand strayed over her breasts, idly caressing. "My father didn't agree. I was kept at home with a tutor for a month."

Arousal slid through her, although she was aching already. "Hardly sounds like a punishment."

"When you grow up surrounded by security who accompany you everywhere, school is a blessed relief. Only on the playing fields and in the classrooms could I feel as if I were like everyone else."

She nodded her understanding. "Being confined to the palace must have been like a jail sentence."

A flick of his hand dismissed the memory. "I learned my lesson, and also to cherish the limited freedoms available to those of royal birth."

Did he count this afternoon with her? "Our experiences weren't so different," she acknowledged. "Both of us had limits placed on us by our heritage." Except that he had grown from his, while she'd allowed fear to limit her.

She wasn't fooling herself that one afternoon of letting go would change years of conditioning, but it was a beginning. The lesson wasn't over yet, she realized as he stroked the length of her body, lower and lower, until he had her arching her back in excitement.

When he came to her, she was open and willing and eager, using her arms and legs to bind him closer, deeper, until all boundaries blurred and she couldn't tell where his ended and hers began.

The next thing she knew, he was rousing her gently. He was dressed but for his headdress and *i'qal,* and had a gold tray in his hands.

Her dreams had been filled with him, or were they only dreams? "You should have woken me."

"It was only a nap, and I enjoyed watching you sleep."

She stretched. "I don't usually sleep during the day. This is your fault."

"I'm sure I'll find a way to make it up to you."

She could think of several. None involved leaving this chamber. To distract herself, she reached for one of the figs glistening on the tray.

He playfully batted her hand away. "Let me. I don't often get the chance to serve food to a beautiful woman."

"And the refrigerator just happened to be well stocked. You realize how calculating this looks?" Her light tone echoed his mood.

"If this were the majlis, I would have to plead guilty."

In the midst of his demanding schedule, he'd taken the time to plan this interlude for her. Confused by the feelings swirling through her mind, she sat up and pulled a section of the rainbow-colored coverlet over herself. If he kept being so thoughtful, she might imagine she was falling in love with him.

Since that was out of the question, she reached for humor. "What's the penalty for seducing a member of your harem?"

"Pleasure beyond her wildest dreams."

"Typical," she retorted, reminded of just how wild those dreams had been. "In every society, the man gets off scot-free."

"You're assuming he wants to."

"What else could he want?"

"Home, family, intimacy with one special person. Men want those things, too."

"Even a sheikh?"

His gaze leveled. "Even the sheikh."

Her question had been general. His answer sounded

personal. She felt her throat dry. Home, family and intimacy also meant giving up control over your life. More
so if you were royal and on duty twenty-four hours a day.
No, she wasn't in love with him. In lust, perhaps, and
what was wrong with that? But never love.

He began to feed her the succulent figs, slivers of melon
and bites of pastry, dabbing her lips with a fine cotton napkin
after each mouthful. Then he gave her sips of sparkling
water from a crystal goblet. As he ministered to her, arousal
began to burn through her anew. She'd never thought of
eating as a sensual experience, but Markaz made it so. "I'd
better get dressed, too," she said, annoyed to feel so
unsteady.

He fixed his headdress in place with the *i'qal.* "There's
no hurry. I have a meeting to attend. Now you know the
way out, you can stay for as long as you wish."

There was only one reason to wait. "Will you come
back after your meeting?"

He shook his head. "Hamal has security concerns to
discuss with me."

Every word proved her belief that Markaz was wrong
for her. But she couldn't keep resentment out of her tone.
"Then I'd better get back to the women. They invited me
to go with them to a restaurant featuring belly dancing."

With his hand on the hidden door control, Markaz
paused. "I'd prefer you to remain in the lodge."

She shook her head. She'd sensed that control of her
life would leave her hands once she gave in to him. Gave
in? She gave. Pure and simple. And took as much in
return. "If I agree to stay here tonight, what comes next?
You order me to remain in my quarters until we return to
Raisa?"

"If necessary," he said through narrowed lips.

"It isn't necessary," she denied. "I know you want to protect me. That was always my father's excuse, too. But I'll be fine. There hasn't been any sign of Business Suit since we got here."

The bed rocked as he sat down beside her and grasped her hand. She wanted to pull away but he held fast, forcing her to meet his glare. "You're wrong. At the souk, one of my mother's attendants saw a man answering Business Suit's description. That's why Fayed was so close at hand. I sent him to look for the man."

Fear tightened her breathing. "Did Fayed find him?"

"No, he got away after Abdl told us you'd been taken."

The implication was clear. "If I'd stayed with the group, Fayed might have caught up with him. Oh, Markaz, I'm sorry. I didn't realize."

"You knew there was danger."

"Yes, but I managed to forget for a short time. I won't forget again," she vowed.

"Good. Then you will remain within the lodge from now on?"

"I'll take greater care," she hedged.

He wasn't fooled. "I want your word that you won't go off on your own, no matter what."

"How can I give my word, when we don't know what might happen next?"

His grip tightened. "Precisely why I require your promise. Don't force me to have you locked in your room under guard."

How many times when she was a child had her father confined her to her room for her own good? "I know there's danger. I'm not stupid. I won't venture away without taking care. But I won't be dictated to like a child."

He stood up. "There will be a guard at your side from now on."

Bitterness forced the words out, "Even when we make love?"

"This room is like a vault. We have no need of guards here."

"They won't be needed anyway. From now on, I don't want you to touch me."

His eyebrows lifted. "Because I consider you precious enough to be worthy of protecting?"

Don't go there, she warned herself. "You make me sound like one of your possessions."

He looked really angry now, and utterly magnificent. "Don't try me too far, Simone."

Not *Sima* now. Strange how bereft the change made her feel. "Which one of you, the lover or the monarch?" And which one had made love to her?

"They cannot be separated."

Her anger deflated. "No, they can't. My mistake." One she wouldn't readily make again, she promised herself.

He made nonsense of the intention by crushing her to him and claiming her mouth. Fueled by anger, this kiss was not in the least gentle, but echoes of their lovemaking churned through her, making her ache.

Needs and wants and desires clashed with her temper. But she wouldn't allow him to sidetrack her. She fought free. "Stop. The price is too high."

He didn't ask what price. She could read the understanding on his chiseled features. "You paid it willingly enough in this bed," he stated.

"Never again."

"Never is a long time."

An eternity of never again allowing herself to know his power and passion. "I can live with that," she lied.

His gaze told her he knew. But he took her at her word. "As you wish. I must attend my meeting now. You will be safe in here, and there will be a guard waiting in the hall of justice when you're ready to return to your room."

So he would have his way. What did she expect? "Your wish is my command, Your Highness."

At her sarcastic tone he looked as if he was about to say more, but instead clamped his mouth into a hard line. In a swish of robes, he went to the wall. Unwilling to watch him leave, she closed her eyes. Moments later, she heard the grating sound as the secret door slid shut behind him.

Dragging the coverlet up to her chin, she lay back. Every part of her felt tender. Her spirit, most of all. Letting him make love to her had been a mistake, granting him power over her beyond his rights as a monarch. She'd known the risks, yet she'd taken them out of simple desire.

No, not simple. Nothing was simple about the way Markaz made her feel. True, she wanted him more than she'd ever wanted any man. Enough to forget her need to run her own life? Yes, she thought bitterly. And now she had to face the consequences.

Well, to hell with that. She was still a free agent. Hearing that Business Suit had been snooping around the souk didn't exactly thrill her, but what could he do to her in the royal lodge? She could identify him as the last person seen with Natalie alive, but he could have established an alibi by now. So why was he following her?

Something nagged at the back of her mind, not for the first time. Had she seen something more without realizing the significance? She thought back to when she'd first seen Business Suit at Al-Qasr. He'd walked toward Natalie's car. Then he'd forced the other woman into the vehicle, before pursuing Simone. Not much to go on.

Impatiently she wound the coverlet around herself like a toga and got up. Much as she hated to admit it, Markaz's insistence on providing her with a guard was starting to make sense. Not that she had any intention of telling the sheikh so. He might get the idea that she liked being ruled by him. And she didn't. She didn't like anything about this arrangement at all.

Her eye was caught by a flash of color on a side table. The mosaic coffer. She picked it up and sprung the gold catch. The bulblets of massage oil called love pearls were nested in velvet alongside two more silver foil pouches. Telling herself he came prepared didn't help. He had said she was the first woman he'd brought here, and she believed him.

Slowly she closed the coffer and put it down, not wanting to think about how he had made her feel. It was time she got out of here and back to the real world.

Chapter 13

Markaz's trusted attendant took good care of the hidden chamber, Simone noticed. Not only was there a supply of refreshments, but when she explored the en suite bathroom, she found everything she needed to freshen up. There was even a selection of lovely new galabias in a closet.

She took her time bathing and changing, and was sipping a glass of chilled water when she tracked down the source of her unease. The planning was too good. Markaz had played her the way a virtuoso plays a violin. She didn't like being so predictable.

Not that she blamed him entirely. She'd been more than ready to be swept off her feet. Would let it happen again in an instant if Markaz came back now and took her in his arms.

Stop this, she ordered herself as the thought of being held by him triggered a surge of response. Hiding in a pleasure dome, wishing he'd come back would get her nowhere. She put down the drink and went to the secret door, remembering to secure her veil before she stepped through.

The antechamber was empty. The majlis sessions were over for the time being, but surely there should have been more activity in the area? The sheikh's promised guard waited at the entrance to the hall of justice. At her approach, the man came to attention sloppily.

Hardly one of Markaz's elite, she thought. Then she recognized Yusef. Or Omar as he called himself. Odd that Markaz should have assigned him to her when he had doubts about the man's loyalty.

"What are you doing here?" she asked. "Did Sheikh Markaz ask you to be my escort?"

"Hamal was supposed to take the duty," the guard said. "But he's investigating a break-in."

"Here at the lodge?" Suddenly she froze with horror. "Is that blood on the floor?" Dear heaven, not Markaz's. "What happened?"

"It is not your concern."

She grabbed his arm, ignoring his recoil of distaste. "If you don't want to find yourself bouncing off these marble walls, you'll answer my question."

He tried to shrug her off. "Control yourself, woman."

Her hold didn't slacken. "Maybe women don't touch men in your world, but where I come from, we do everything men do. Including wipe the floor with anyone giving us a hard time."

The guard's eyes narrowed. "You wouldn't dare."

"Care to put me to the test?"

He looked thunderous, but one glance at the fire in her eyes silenced further argument. "When the majlis session ended, an intruder hid in this chamber and attacked the sheikh," he said sullenly.

Her veil fluttered in time with her labored breathing. She released the man's arm. "Is Markaz all right?"

"He fought the man off. The blood mostly belongs to the intruder."

Omar sounded suspiciously regretful, she thought. Something more was going on. No matter what had happened, she doubted that Markaz would allow Omar to guard her.

"Was the sheikh injured."

"His personal physician is attending him now," Omar said.

While she was pampering herself in the pleasure pavilion, Markaz had been fighting possibly for his life. She could hardly believe it. "Did Hamal catch the intruder?"

"He escaped into the Lost Quarter. Hamal and his men went after him."

Now she knew why the lodge seemed unusually quiet. The guards were either attending Markaz or chasing the intruder. If it was Business Suit, he was more slippery than an eel, she thought. Had he been looking for her when he was tackled by Markaz?

She drew herself up. "Take me to the sheikh at once." The dark stains on the floor had shaken her. She would have no peace until she saw for herself that Markaz was all right.

The guard shook his head. "My orders are to escort you to your room and maintain watch outside until relieved."

"I'm giving you new orders."

The guard's lip curled. "I don't take orders from the spawn of traitors."

A chill ran through her. "So you do know who I am."

"Everyone in the royal household knows. You are the

daughter of cowards who abandoned their country rather than change their wrong beliefs."

She refused to be drawn into defending her parents, when there was so much more at stake. "I insist you take me to Sheikh Markaz right now."

"Such touching concern. Too bad it is misplaced. You will come with me."

She folded her arms. "I'll go nowhere except to see the sheikh."

The delay gnawed at her, fueling her fear that Markaz was more badly injured than she was being told. She had to see, to know.

She tried to sidestep the guard, but he blocked her way. For days she'd schemed to get the chance to talk to Yusef. Now she struggled to find the words to reach him. "When you were a teenager, my mother gave you a home and cared about you. She's alone and ill, but she still cares. She sent me to make sure you're all right."

"Why should your mother care about a soldier called Omar Zirhan?" he asked.

"We both know your real name is Yusef al Hasa and you're my half uncle. What I don't know is which side you're on."

"You are mistaken," he said coldly.

This was getting her nowhere. "Suit yourself. Just take me back to my room." There she could seek out Amal and try to get news of Markaz.

"So you can prepare yourself for your lover, the sheikh?" Omar asked nastily.

She drew herself up. "What I do is not your concern."

"You should have thought of that before you spent the afternoon in the sheikh's bed."

"How do you know how I spent the afternoon?"

He gestured toward the retreat at the back of the hall. "You and the sheikh were alone in that room for a considerable time. Under our old laws, you would have been stoned for such wanton behavior."

"Then thank goodness the old laws no longer apply."

"For the moment."

"What are you saying? That you're working to bring back the old laws?"

"I'm only a humble guard. How can I influence the law?"

"You could if you're still in league with the rebels. That's it, isn't it? You worked your way into the sheikh's service so you could sabotage the reform process from the inside. Markaz was right, you're still loyal to the rebel cause."

He turned aside, dodging her gaze. "I am Omar Zirhan, local hero and servant of His Royal Highness, Sheikh Markaz bin Kemal al Nazaari."

And a double agent. Her mother would be heartbroken if she ever learned the truth. Not that Simone could tell her. Better to let her think Yusef had vanished without trace. In a way, it was true. "You realize I have to tell the sheikh what I know?" she said.

"You won't get the chance." Apparently to himself, he said, "Take her."

Out of the shadows emerged a second man, also in guard's uniform. Before she could react, she was grabbed and her arms jerked behind her. She felt rope cut into her wrists as her hands were tied. "What is this?" she demanded, trying not to sound as frightened as she felt.

"You'll have answers soon enough, not that they'll do you much good."

"The sheikh already suspects you. If you disappear with me, you'll confirm his suspicions. Your plans, whatever they are, will be finished."

Yusef advanced on her. "I'm not going to disappear. You are."

"No," she protested, but her cries were stifled when her veil was pushed into her mouth as a gag, secured by a scarf tied around her head. She was blind as well as silenced.

Although she fought to put her martial arts training to good use, there wasn't much she could do tied and blind-folded against two strong men.

She felt herself being hustled along a corridor, her feet barely touching the ground. Why didn't somebody see her and report what was happening? Were they all out tracking the intruder, or attending to Markaz? She didn't like to think Yusef's people had more support than the sheikh guessed.

In fury she kicked out, choosing her target from the man's grip on her arm. She was rewarded by a cry of pain and an oath in Arabic. Her earthy response was muffled by the gag as she kicked out at her other side.

This time she wasn't so lucky. Yusef had learned from his friend's experience. Her kick met empty air and was followed by an openhanded blow to the side of her head. Dazed, she stumbled, but was held up and dragged along until she got her feet under her again.

Where did they think they were taking her? Surely they couldn't abduct her from a well-guarded royal lodge without being challenged?

But it seemed they didn't have to. She was pulled to a stop, then forced down onto something that felt like a bed. Not a bed, a stretcher. Straps were fastened over her so she couldn't move. A blanket was draped across her and she felt the stretcher being lifted. Into a vehicle? The suspicion was confirmed when she heard a door slam and an engine start.

The straps binding her to the stretcher made for a jolting ride with her hands tied behind her. She slowed her breathing, trying to control her panic. They still had to pass through the main gates.

Moments later she heard a sentry challenge the vehicle. But her elation was short lived. She heard one of them men say they'd collected the sick woman and were transporting her to the hospital in Karama as arranged.

"Poor Amal collapsed when she heard about the attempt on the sheikh's life," the other man added.

She tried to scream a denial, but only pulled the veil deeper into her mouth, making her choke. The sentry made a joke with the driver, accepting Amal as their passenger without checking. One veiled woman looked much like another. Damn these concealing garments. The sooner Markaz outlawed them, the better.

Markaz. Her despair grew as she imagined him hurt or worse. She reined in her errant imagination. The best way she could help him was to stay calm and learn what she could about where she was taken. She couldn't let herself think about what would happen to her when they got there.

She heard the main gate open and the vehicle start up again. The wheels bouncing over a cobbled surface added to her discomfort, but helped to orientate her. They were following the main road to Karama. Not the Lost Quarter, she prayed. She might have desert blood, but she was under no illusions that she could survive in such a hostile environment, even supposing she managed to escape. At least in the city there was the chance of help.

She felt the sleeve of her galabia being thrust back. Automatically she jerked away from the touch.

"Stay still," one of her abductors ordered.

Fighting harder, she felt herself straddled, pinned down by the man's weight. From the front of the vehicle, she heard a laugh then Yusef's voice. "Don't enjoy yourself too much back there."

Her attacker growled. "You think this is fun? She fights like a tiger."

"No wonder she caught the sheikh's eye. Do you think Western women are as uninhibited as they say?"

Her attacker shifted above her. "Maybe we'll get the chance to find out."

"Don't let Sozar hear you say that," the driver retorted. "From the way he's followed her every move, he probably has her picked out for himself."

Hearing the name, she stilled. Could Sozar be the man she called Business Suit? What did he want with her? What was she to him? A hand clamped over her arm. She tried to pull free, but was held fast. She felt a sting and a cold sensation of something being injected into her arm, then her attacker climbed off her.

As whatever he'd given her took effect, the ride became even more surreal. She felt as if she were on a ship plowing through a heaving swell. Nausea made her stomach roll. She breathed shallowly in an attempt to keep her stomach contents where they belonged.

Within a short time she felt her limbs become heavy and unresponsive. She struggled to stop her eyelids sliding shut. With the blindfold in place, she couldn't be sure when she lost the battle.

"With respect, Your Highness, this would be easier if you would hold still."

Markaz frowned at the doctor. "Is all this fuss necessary? The wound is only slight."

Dr. Rakha glared back. "Any less slight and you would be in hospital getting stitches instead of being taped back together in the infirmary by your kindly royal physician."

Grudgingly Markaz relaxed his arm. "It's bad enough being attacked in my own hall of justice, without an unnecessary visit to the hospital."

"I thought you'd see it my way."

As the doctor cleaned and dried the gash marring his forearm, Markaz averted his eyes. He wasn't a big fan of bloodshed, especially his own. The attacker had come at him from behind, having concealed himself behind the heavy drapes possibly for hours since the last session of the majlis ended.

Hearing a slight sound, Markaz had spun around, thinking that Simone had followed him out of the antechamber. Seeing the knife, he'd instinctively thrown up his arm. His robes had absorbed some of the blow, but where his sleeve had slid back, the blade had sliced along his forearm. Markaz could still see the killing fury in the man's eyes as he wielded the knife.

He'd made sure his attacker had suffered, getting in a couple of blows that had crunched bones. Then he'd slipped on his own blood and the attacker had moved in to end the fight. Luckily for Markaz, Hamal had arrived at the hall to consult with the sheikh, and the intruder had fled.

Thank goodness Simone had been safely within the soundproofed chamber, Markaz thought. Imagining her hurt was worse than the pain of his injury. But Hamal would see her to her quarters when the crisis was past.

The security chief had wasted no time setting up roadblocks around the royal lodge, but no arrests had been reported so far. Markaz had the feeling there wouldn't be any, either. The intruder had more lives than a cat. How had he managed to get into the enclave unseen? Only one answer made sense. He'd had help from the inside.

"Whoever you're ready to punch, I hope it isn't me," the doctor said.

Markaz unclenched the fist he'd unconsciously made, then swore as he felt a fierce stinging sensation.

"Sorry," Dr. Rakha said. "You shouldn't move. Benzoin touching an open wound can sting like the devil."

Markaz wouldn't put it past the man to let it happen to remind the sheikh of his mortality. Rakha had been the royal physician for most of Markaz's life, and didn't take kindly to being told how to do his job. "Get on with it," Markaz growled.

"As you wish, Your Highness."

"Your groveling doesn't fool me. You're enjoying having me at your mercy."

The doctor raised an eyebrow. "I wouldn't dream of fooling Your Highness. Or of groveling, for that matter. But next time you decide to have a run-in with a knife of unknown hygiene, could you do it on my day off?"

Tempted to tell him every day from now on might well fall into that category, Markaz restrained himself. Rakha loved nothing better than verbal sparring with his boss, but today Markaz wasn't in the mood. Apart from the pain of his wound, he had the dilemma of what to do about Simone.

He was afraid she was starting to mean far more to him than was wise. But he'd known the risk when he took her to the secret room. He'd promised himself never to take a woman there unless he intended to marry her.

He didn't intend to marry Simone. Did he?

"Ouch," he yelped, jerking his arm away from the doctor.

Rakha straightened, surgical tape dangling from his fingers. "You're not making this easy. I hope she's worth it."

Markaz eyed him sharply. "I was thinking about affairs of state."

The doctor bent to his work again, cutting one of the strips of tape and folding a quarter of it over lengthwise. "Sure you were," he murmured. "The hidden chamber is tailor-made for discussing such matters."

The sheikh felt his face heat. "What are you talking about?"

"I saw the two of you going into your room off the justice hall. You weren't seen again until the intruder showed up a couple of hours later. That's a long time to spend in an unadorned anteroom."

Rakha attached a piece of the prepared tape to each side of the knife wound, then reached for a surgical needle and thread.

Markaz made an effort not to flinch. "I thought you said this wouldn't need stitches."

"This is only to cinch the tape and bring the skin edges together so the wound heals cleanly. If you prefer, I can tie a lock of hair from a horse's tail around your arm to cure it," he said, referring to an ancient piece of Nazaari folklore.

Markaz finally rose to the bait. "You would be more familiar with that end of a horse than I would."

"Ah, the patient's spirit shows signs of recovery," the doctor said. He efficiently stitched the tape in place. Markaz felt a tug of pain as the edges of the wound were brought together. "You were talking about the hidden chamber," the doctor prompted as he snipped the thread.

Rakha was the one who'd brought up the chamber, but Markaz didn't think he should say so while the other man was wielding surgical instruments. "How do you know about the room?" he demanded.

The doctor looked up from filling a syringe. "Your mother told me about it when she was expecting you. Don't worry, I've told no one else. Patient confidentiality."

And his own strict ethics, Markaz thought. Rakha might be irritatingly argumentative, but he was the finest doctor in Nazaar. Caring for the royal family was his whole life. He had never married, making him an unlikely advisor on love, but he did know how to hold his tongue when it counted. "In theory, would you say that a man taking a woman to such a place was significant?" Markaz asked.

Rakha approached him with the hypodermic. "Strictly in theory, I'd say it suggests that he's pretty serious about her."

"Would that be good or bad?"

"Theoretically, it should be good, if both parties feel the same way."

"What about other factors, like the future of the country? In theory," Markaz added.

Rakha swabbed the sheikh's upper arm. "A man can't always run his life for the good of his country."

"Even if it's his duty?"

"We're still talking theoretically?" When Markaz nodded, Rakha went on, "Not all women are like Natalie. A few come to love Nazaar as much as those of us who were born here. Like your mother, for instance."

They'd moved from theoretical to personal, Markaz noticed. The doctor was a smooth operator. "My mother is an unusual woman."

"So is Simone. Although I suspect I'm not telling you anything you don't know."

After their afternoon in the secret chamber, Markaz couldn't argue. But mind-shattering as their joining had been, she was special in other ways, too. His mother had told him how interested she'd been in the Nazaari crafts she was shown. And she'd taken Amal's advice, striving to fit in with local custom. Her concern for young, love-struck Bibi was also admirable.

Simone's keen mind and interest in everything around her were key to her nature. She wanted to learn, to experience, to grow. All qualities he admired as much as her unselfconscious beauty and passion. Like him, she also worked hard and was a capable administrator. He'd visited her Web site and seen for himself the attention to detail she applied to her business affairs. She hadn't let that slip despite being in danger since coming to his country.

She had courage, too, demonstrated when she put her life at risk to get Natalie's message to Markaz.

Markaz felt his heart grow heavy. He knew Simone was attracted to him. In his arms, she'd exploded like a fire-cracker. But she wasn't willing to subject herself to any man's rule. And until he could bring in the rest of his reforms, she would have little choice. Nazaari law placed women in the subordinate role they'd occupied for thousands of years. Even Markaz couldn't change that over-night.

Dr. Rakha held up the syringe and tapped it to exclude air bubbles. "What potion are you preparing now?" Markaz asked.

"Tetanus booster shot. Wouldn't want you coming down with something from contact with that knife."

Markaz looked away as Rakha gave him the shot, then rubbed the spot. "Can I get back to running the country now?"

"You need to rest. You've lost a lot of blood."

"I've been resting while you practiced your folk medicine on me."

"Well, rest some more. Doctor's orders. Those horse tails take time to work."

Markaz shrugged his shirt back on, aware of his arm throbbing in spite of Rakha's painkillers. Before he could lever himself off the table, Hamal came in. The security chief nodded to the doctor, then came to attention in front of Markaz.

"Did you locate the intruder?"

"No, Your Highness. We searched every inch of the lodge and grounds and set up a ring of roadblocks, but he got clean away." The security man hesitated, as if unsure how to go on.

Markaz forgot about his arm. "Is there something else?"

"Yes, Your Highness. After you were attacked, Amal collapsed in shock and was taken to the hospital by ambulance. Or so we thought."

"What do you mean?"

"According to the men at the western roadblock, two of our own guards were driving the ambulance."

Dr. Rakha stopped putting away his instruments and tilted his head. "Isn't that unusual?"

Hamal nodded. "The ambulance should have been driven by medics from the hospital. But because they were our own men, they were allowed through the roadblock unchallenged. The sentries checked the back of the ambulance, but didn't disturb the female patient."

Markaz's fingers stilled on the fastenings of his shirt. "Are you saying they abducted Amal?"

Hamal looked as if he would like to be anywhere else. "No, Your Highness. It turns out that she was reading in her room at the time of the incident."

A chill swept through Markaz. "Then who was the woman in the ambulance?"

"Amal fears it was Sima al Hasa. She hasn't been seen since the attack on you."

When he'd left her in the secret chamber, Markaz thought. Pain throbbed through his arm like a second heartbeat, but he ignored it, berating himself for leaving her alone. He'd been sure she was safe, guarded by his own men. "Didn't you escort her back to her room as I ordered?" he asked Hamal.

The security chief glanced down. "No, sir. When you were injured, I couldn't leave you to take care of the princess."

Markaz couldn't keep the chill out of his tone. "Who did you delegate as her escort?"

"Omar Zirhan, Your Highness."

"Even though you know he isn't completely trustworthy?"

"He was the only available man. The rest of your personal guards were searching for the intruder."

Markaz couldn't fault the man for doing his duty, but he wished fervently that Hamal had been more conscientious. "Where is Omar now?"

"According to the men guarding the roadblock, Omar was one of the two men driving the ambulance."

This time Markaz swore crudely and with feeling. "I might as well have handed her over to the rebels personally."

Dr. Rakha came and placed a hand on his shoulder. "This isn't your doing. You mustn't blame yourself."

"If anyone's to blame, it's me," Hamal said. "I failed in my duty."

The sheikh shook his head. "Nobody failed. The rebels are smarter than we expected, and it seems they have more than one person working inside my household."

"I will not rest until these traitors are rooted out," Hamal vowed.

"I agree, but they aren't our main concern right now. We need to find out where the rebels have taken Simone—Sima—and get to her before she comes to harm." He didn't add that he feared they may already be too late.

Chapter 14

When she awoke, the first thing Simone noticed was the silence. A sea of dunes and a light wind whipping up the sand swallowed the sound of the motor. Swallowed everything. Her head ached appallingly, and her vision took its time clearing. But at least the blindfold had been removed and she could try to see where she was.

She was in a Jeep being driven by Omar. Another man in a guard's uniform shared the backseat with her, a rifle held across his lap in silent warning. She couldn't see the necessity. Where could she run to out here?

They hadn't taken the road to Karama, she realized. While she'd been unconscious, her abductors must have switched the ambulance for the Jeep and headed away from the city, into the desert.

As her vision improved, all she could see was bleached white sand. There were no buildings and no discernible road, only the faint tracks left by some other vehicle, perhaps days before.

Occasionally they passed one of the unnamed sandstone bridges that attracted tourists to the area. Today under a full blue sky and baking heat, there were no tourists and no sense of the journey nearing an end. How long had they been traveling? Her watch had been damaged at some point, so she had no way to tell.

She licked her dry lips. Her veil was in place but no longer being used as a gag. And her hands were now tied in front of her, hidden by her robe, perhaps to make her status as a prisoner less apparent to casual observers. "Can I have some water?" she asked the man with the rifle.

Omar looked over his shoulder. "Noor doesn't like speaking English."

She repeated her request in Arabic, startling the guard. Grudgingly he uncapped a flask and handed it to her. She raised her veil enough to gulp the tepid fluid. At least they weren't going to kill her right away, or they wouldn't waste precious water on her. Now there was a cheering thought.

The journey dragged on. Her spirits rose briefly at the sight of a desert community living in homes dug out of a sandstone hillside. The inhabitants looked curiously at the Jeep, but kept on about their affairs.

She debated calling out to them for help, but the rifle stopped her. If Omar and his friend would condone an attack on the sheikh, they wouldn't balk at shooting innocent bystanders. She'd have to get out of this on her own.

Did Markaz know she'd been abducted? Were his men out looking for her by now? Or was he more badly injured than she'd been told? She had to survive so she could assure herself that Markaz was all right. They had no future together, but she needed to know he was well.

200   *Desert Justice*

She didn't regret letting him make love to her, especially now. If she was to die soon, she had soared with him to heights of passion few people experienced. The imprint of his mouth felt vivid on hers still, and closing her eyes brought back the sensation of his hard body aligned with hers. The hunger to feel his arms around her was almost palpable.

Opening her eyes, she blinked furiously. Wasting moisture on tears was pointless. She had chosen not to subjugate herself to Markaz's rule, as she would have to do to live in his world. Passion wasn't enough. They needed more in common for a relationship to work.

Who was she kidding? They had a great deal in common. Not only in bed, but beyond it. She shared his interest in the world around him, as well as a passion for Nazaari culture. She hadn't been raised here but the longer she stayed, the more she felt the pull of her ancestry. Marrying and having a family here seemed all too possible.

At the thought of having Markaz's children, she placed her bound hands over her stomach in instinctive self-protection, surprised to feel so regretful that nothing could come of their lovemaking. She'd joked to Drew that the spring on her biological clock must be broken. To find it ticking so loudly now was unexpected.

She not only wanted Markaz, she wanted his baby. In her book, you only had a child with a man you loved. Yet she couldn't love Markaz. In terms of suitable men, he wasn't even on her radar. But she couldn't deny how she felt.

Since she wasn't going to solve the dilemma now, she turned her attention to the landscape. Among the white dunes, rust-colored hills capped with smooth, pale sandstone began to arise. They increased in height until they formed a canyon enclosing a hidden valley a couple of miles wide. Too tense to enjoy the beauty of the scenery, she wondered how anyone would ever find her here.

They approached the far end of the canyon and Simone spotted some black marks on the horizon. As they got closer, she saw a palm-studded spring surrounded by large tents made out of goat-hair fabric, branches and rope, the only signs of civilization for miles around.

In a series of roped-off corrals, men were working out under the relentless sun. They were a fearsome sight in khaki robes, with bandoliers of ammunition, daggers at their waists, some with rifles slung over their shoulders.

One group was on horseback, shooting at targets at full gallop, the shots echoing off the cliff walls. Others, shirt-less and bronzed, were engaged in hand-to-hand combat while leaders shouted orders and comments.

This had to be the rebels' training camp.

Omar steered the Jeep toward a line of stationary vehicles streaked with desert sand. Under a camouflage roof made of netting, she saw larger armored vehicles, one carrying what looked like a missile launcher. Her heart lurched. These men were preparing for war. With Markaz and his government?

Not that she would get the chance to warn him. The rebels wouldn't risk bringing her to their secret stronghold if they intended to let her leave.

Before they'd rolled to a complete stop, Noor jumped out, rifle held ready. Omar came around to her side of the Jeep. "Out," he ordered.

She met his gaze unflinchingly. "You know these people intend to kill me?"

He lowered his eyes. "All war has casualties."

"If this is war, and that's moot, I'm not part of it," she argued. "But I am your own flesh and blood, your half brother's child. How can you condone what you know is going to happen?"

"I didn't say I condone it. Like all soldiers, I do my duty."

"What's the holdup?" the other man demanded.

Omar gestured with his thumb. "Get out. No more talk."

On jellylike legs, she climbed out. For a moment, Omar had sounded almost regretful at what he was doing to her. Wishful thinking, she decided. Noor prodded her with the barrel. "Move it. Sozar is waiting."

Omar pushed the rifle aside. "That isn't necessary. She isn't going anywhere."

"Except to your bunk," jeered the other man. "You'd better get in line. Women are in short supply in this camp," he added for Simone's benefit.

She refused to give in to fear. Once she did, all hope was lost. She would get out of this, although the men pausing in their training to whistle and call out lewd comments eroded her assurance.

A legacy of her martial arts training was the instinct to absorb as much detail of her surroundings as she could. The place wasn't as big as she'd first thought. Maybe a dozen men were in training, others cleaning weapons. Several excitable Arab mares milled in a corral nearby. One man who leered at her as she passed was feeding wires into traditional Nazaari pottery flagons, the kind used to hold olive oil. He was making bombs that wouldn't be recognized as such until they exploded, she thought, her blood chilling.

By the time she was ordered to wait outside one of the tents, she could feel herself trembling. Locking her knees, she stared straight ahead. Whoever waited for her inside wasn't going to see her quaking.

She wasn't surprised to find Business Suit seated on the far side of a trestle table, conferring with an aide. This time he wore a sheikh's robes and a black *mishlah* and headdress. In the robes he looked even more formidable than he had in Western dress. Looking closer, she saw he had bruises on his face and his forearm was bandaged as if he'd been in a recent fight. Her spirits lifted a little. If this man was the intruder, Markaz had made sure he didn't escape unscathed.

When the man looked up, his obsidian eyes bored into her as if she were a specimen being prepared to go under a microscope.

Ripping away her veil, she marched to the table. "I assume you're Sozar?" That was the name Noor had mentioned.

Her audacity left the aide looking horrified. "This is His Royal Highness Sozar bin Kemal al Frayan, rightful ruler of Nazaar," he said, sounding aggrieved.

Sozar made a gesture of dismissal. "Thank you, Salman. I'm afraid our guest isn't as impressed as you are. Please leave us alone."

As the aide gathered up his papers and left, her mind raced. *Bin Kemal* meant son of Kemal. Surely not the Kemal who was also Markaz's father? Sozar looked to be several years older than Markaz. Could he possibly be an illegitimate son? If so, what was his claim to the throne?

"Sit," Sozar ordered. When she complied, Sozar smiled without warmth. "I see you are working things out. Yes, Kemal bin Aziz al Nazaari was also my father."

"But his eldest son died."

"His eldest known son. I was born of a youthful indiscretion, and never acknowledged. Now my time has come."

"Did the old sheikh know you existed?"

She'd hit a nerve, she saw when his expression darkened. "My mother decided not to tell him. She left me to be taken in by strangers."

"Then surely your mother is to blame for your situation, not Markaz and his family?"

Sozar's fist slammed down, making everything on the table dance. "This is not your concern."

"By having me abducted, you made it my concern."

"You eluded my previous efforts to corner you."

Her chin lifted. "You haven't cornered me now. You may hold me captive, but I won't help you to bring Markaz down."

"Because you are his lover?"

She didn't bother denying the truth. "Because he's right and you're wrong. The people won't be dragged back to the Dark Ages. Nazaar must progress."

Sozar's mouth twisted into a sneer. "Under his rule, I suppose."

"Yes, since your only alternative seems to be armed insurrection."

Sozar surged to his feet. "If you were a man, I'd kill you."

"You'll kill me anyway, so I may as well speak my mind."

A look of reluctant admiration crossed his features. "I can see why Markaz finds you alluring, if you're as fiery in bed as out of it. A question worth exploring later."

If he so much as touched her, he was a dead man, she resolved. "You didn't bring me here for that. What do you really want?"

"You underestimate your charms, madam. But I do have another reason. I want to know what you did with the ring you were given by the woman you aided at Al-Qasr."

"What use is a class ring to you anyway?" she dissembled, hoping to learn more.

He didn't disappoint her. "The ring contains the code to operate a new weapon developed between the Americans and a group of Nazaari scientists."

Natalie must have been delivering the code to Markaz, Simone reasoned. As she'd suspected, the ring was much more than a means of identification. Were the rebels going to steal the weapon and use the code to activate it? Somehow she had to warn Markaz. "Then it's as well I lost the ring," she stated.

"I am acquainted with an expert in clinical hypnosis who can be here by tomorrow. He'll get the information from you."

She set her jaw. "I won't cooperate."

Sozar's smile was pure evil. "You won't have to. This man is a former police detective, disgraced because he used unscrupulous interrogation methods. He will use whatever techniques get results. I should warn you, he enjoys his work."

In spite of herself, Simone shuddered. The most recent attack on Markaz must have been an attempt to get to the ring. When that failed, Sozar had snatched her. She had no illusions that she could avoid betraying Markaz under duress. She only hoped he would forgive her if he ever found out.

Markaz paced and tried to ignore the throbbing in his arm. A citywide search had failed to locate Simone. The ambulance taking her away from the royal lodge had been found abandoned on a route leading out of the city. The only possible conclusion was that she'd been driven into the desert in a different vehicle.

He spun to face Hamal who'd delivered the news about the ambulance. "Assemble a squad of our most trusted men, including you and Fayed. We're going into the Lost Quarter. We can't fly in without alerting the rebels and putting Simone at greater risk, so we'll do this the hard way."

"I must protest your personal involvement in such a mission, Your Highness. The risk is too great. Let me lead the mission. Your people need you alive and well."

And I need Simone more than the people need me, Markaz thought, finally accepting the truth. Against all reason, he was in love with her. If he couldn't have her at his side, he wouldn't be a fit monarch anyway. "You have your orders," he told Hamal.

Less than two hours later, the small convoy was ready to roll.

Few tracks led into the desert so it wasn't difficult to follow the most recent ones. At a family compound dug into the hillside, he told Fayed to ask if anyone had seen a woman traveling with two men. An elderly villager admitted she had. When Markaz pressed a reward into her hand, she looked stunned and tried to kiss the sheikh's hand in return. He shook her off. "You've earned the reward by serving your country." And its ruler, but he kept the thought to himself.

"What is your plan after we locate Simone?" Fayed asked when one of the cars overheated, forcing a stop in the meager shade of a massive sand dune.

Markaz drank from a canteen then handed the container to Fayed. "That depends on what we find." The thought of stumbling across Simone's body, as they'd done Natalie's, filled him with horror.

Fayed's expression showed that he guessed what was

going through the sheikh's mind. "From the old woman's description, she's being kept alive, but for how long?"

She would be all right until she'd provided the information the rebels needed, Markaz thought. He had to get to her before then.

"They could hope you'll do what you're doing, and try to rescue her," Fayed pointed out.

"You think this is a trap?"

His friend nodded. "Hamal's squad is handpicked. We could locate Simone and bring her out without risking you."

"If your wife was the captive, would you agree to remain in safety?"

Fayed gave him a considering look. "We think alike, you and I."

"Then you understand why I have to lead this mission?"

"I believe so."

Reading his friend's expression, Markaz smiled thinly. "But you don't think our relationship has a snowball's chance in the desert?"

"Simone is a remarkable woman."

A ringing endorsement from his normally taciturn bodyguard. Markaz clasped the big man's arm. "This love business is hell, isn't it?"

He was rewarded by one of Fayed's rare smiles. "Closer to heaven, when it works."

Markaz levered himself away from the car, wincing as his injured arm protested. "Let's move out."

Less than two hours later they approached a region pockmarked with vast canyons. Some had never been fully explored. At Hamal's signal the convoy halted and the security chief jumped down to study tire marks in the sand. "I recommend proceeding on foot from here," he told Markaz.

Markaz nodded. "If the rebels are using the *siq* as a

stronghold, they'll have sentries to warn of a convoy approaching." They might also kill Simone if, indeed, she was being held there. He wasn't about to put her at greater risk than was absolutely necessary.

For the same reason, Markaz ordered Hamal and his squad to follow at a distance while he and Fayed went ahead on foot. He let Hamal argue all the reasons why the sheikh shouldn't put himself in danger, then cut off the protestations with a sharp gesture. "Enough. I have decided."

He saw Hamal exchange glances with Fayed. Without knowing how the sheikh felt about Simone, Hamal probably thought Markaz had lost his mind. Perhaps he had. He only knew that nothing would keep him back here when the woman he loved was in danger.

Night fell quickly in the desert. The farther he and Fayed pushed into the canyon, the darker it became until the velvet sky was crowded with stars and the silence pressed against their eardrums. The moon was a thin crescent through a haze of light cloud overhead, turning the dunes a glowing white where they leaned against the cliff walls.

Aware of how Markaz felt about Simone, Fayed didn't argue his boss's insistence on leading the way. He'd make a good best man at the wedding, the sheikh thought.

Imagining Simone in lavishly embroidered wedding robes, her luscious lips tantalizing behind a gauzy veil, set Markaz's pulse pounding. He pictured himself moving the veil aside and kissing her, then forced the vision away as too distracting. First he had to find her.

"Sentry up ahead."

Fayed's whispered warning had Markaz melting against the cliff wall. He gestured his question. How many?

Fayed held up one finger and Markaz smiled grimly. Only one? The rebels were overconfident. He looked around, spotting another sentry on a cliff top. Markaz pointed the man out to Fayed, gesturing that he would take the nearest man. His friend nodded, and silently started to climb in the direction of the other sentry.

The cliff provided good cover and Markaz was able to get within striking range before the man realized he was there. A blow to his windpipe stifled the sentry's cry and he folded like a broken doll. A short time later he was tied up and stowed in a cleft in the rock, and Markaz was changing into the khaki robes.

"Eat. You must keep up your strength," Sozar urged Simone.

They sat beside a blazing fire. The men tore into plates of grilled meat and couscous, washing them down with local beer and traditional date and fig liquors. She'd refused the drinks and had barely touched the food in front of her. "I'm not hungry."

"One should not refuse desert hospitality."

She held up her hands still tied in front of her. Sozar had loosened the bonds so she could eat, but had refused her plea to untie her altogether. "Hospitality implies a free choice."

Sozar wiped his fingers. "Your right to choose ended when you sided with Markaz."

"Why are you so jealous of him?"

He swigged liquor from a bottle. "Why shouldn't I be jealous? He had the best of everything while I had to drag myself up from poverty, being beaten for every minor mistake by a stepfather who hated the bastard child his wife had insisted on taking in."

"Why didn't your birth mother tell the old sheikh about you?"

At first she thought he wasn't going to answer, then he said, "She couldn't."

"I don't understand."

As the liquor took effect, Sozar's words became slurred and thick with anger. "When Kemal was a prince in his teens, my mother was working as a nurse in the household of a princess he admired. Kemal arranged a meeting, but the princess changed her mind and sent the nurse to tell Kemal she wouldn't meet him."

Sozar drank from the bottle, ignoring the liquor dribbling down his hand. "My stupid mother had fallen in love with Kemal herself. Wearing her mistress's robes and veil, she posed as the princess and permitted Kemal to seduce her, insisting on darkness to protect her secret. She was able to slip away while he was asleep, so that he never learned her true identity. They took precautions, but inexperience made them careless."

"Couldn't she tell him she was pregnant?"

"She was afraid he would hate her for deceiving him and have her deported. She kept quiet because she wanted to stay near him."

"Being young and foolish is hardly a crime," Simone observed.

"Unless you're a foreign woman working in Nazaar."

"Don't you see that's the kind of situation Markaz is trying to change."

Sozar's enraged look told her she'd said the wrong thing. "He's thirty-eight years too late. My mother panicked and tried to get rid of me, but she'd left it too long. I was born alive, and survived against all odds."

"Didn't she know you were alive?"

"She was admitted under a false name and left immediately after the procedure." His mouth twisted. "She didn't wait around to find out what had happened to me."

"Then how did you discover who your father was?"

He downed another swallow of liquor. "The medication she was given had loosened her tongue and she'd confided in one of the staff at the clinic. The staff member later persuaded her husband to take me in. Whenever I displeased him, he taunted me about being the sheikh's unwanted bastard. One day I asked my adoptive mother why he said such things, and she told me what she knew."

His mouth curved into a cruel smile. "I see I've shocked you. Good. Now you understand my drive to reclaim my birthright."

"I agree that Kemal was as culpable as your mother. A pregnancy takes two people. But none of this is Markaz's fault."

Sozar laughed. "He doesn't even know I exist. But he will. When you reveal what you saw on the ring, I'll have the code to his new weapon. I can take what is rightfully mine."

And tomorrow, his hypnotist would drag the code out of her mind. She had to escape before then. Perishing in the desert was preferable to letting Sozar use her to unleash his bitterness on Markaz and his people.

She let herself sway. "I feel dizzy. I need to rest."

Leering and increasingly affected by liquor, he patted the cushion beside him. "You can rest against me. The evening's entertainment is about to begin."

She had no interest in any show. And even less in getting closer to him. "The dizziness will pass. I'll be fine."

A few feet away from the campfire, a space had been

cleared. She saw why as a group of rebels rode full tilt into the camp, yelling and shooting into the air.

In the firelight, the riders' bodies gleamed and their expressions were ferocious. Her breath caught as their Arab mounts stopped dead in their tracks then spun on their hocks and darted off again in a ballet as abandoned as it was spectacular.

They were engaged in what looked like a primitive game of polo, although no polo she'd ever seen involved firing guns, throwing them into the air and catching them again while standing or kneeling in the saddle and at a full gallop. Some of the players juggled lances longer than their horses.

Combined with the cheers of the watchers, the noise was unbelievable. She saw Sozar lean drunkenly forward, engrossed in the spectacle.

Through the chaos she glimpsed two riderless mares, most likely replacements for any animals that became injured. Straight away she saw her chance.

Although she muttered about needing to visit the bathroom, Sozar focused drunkenly on the game and didn't respond. She slipped between the tents and edged toward the tethered horses. Hampered by her tied hands, she'd covered less than half the distance when she found a rifle leveled at her.

"Yusef, it's me. Don't shoot."

He gestured with the rifle. "Get back to Sozar."

"I can't. Tomorrow he's going to have me hypnotized to get information. I'd rather take my chances in the desert."

"You'll die out there."

"Better than what Sozar has in store for me."

Agonizing seconds later, the rifle barrel pointed skyward. "If you run, I'll shoot."

Praying she hadn't misread Yusef's message, she took off for the horses at a run. A shot whistled over her head, the report lost among the bedlam. Tears streaked her cheeks and she lifted her tied hands to wipe them away. So blood was thicker than water after all. Omar had taken a long time in choosing his family over his cause, but she wasn't about to question his decision.

Only a few yards remained between her and the horses when one of the contestants suddenly wheeled his mount around and rode straight at her, his cries bloodcurdling. The lower half of his face was swathed in a scarf. All she could see were a pair of blazing black eyes reflecting the firelight, and the lance he held as if he meant to run her through.

As death thundered toward her, she couldn't make herself move or look away. He was almost upon her when he threw the lance aside, leaned out of the saddle and hooked her off her feet.

Too winded to scream, she was thrown into the saddle in front of him. Then he hauled the horse's head around and they plunged into the night, away from the din of the contest.

Only the man's hold kept her upright. The powdery sand churned beneath the horse's hooves and she would have gone under them, had she slipped off. Her bound hands left her no way to save herself. But her abductor made sure she didn't slip. She'd have bruises tomorrow from his iron grip, if she survived this wild ride.

Chapter 15

Gradually the racket from the rebel camp faded behind them. The horse's pace didn't slacken, but Simone found herself adjusting to the rhythm and felt less in danger of hurtling off.

Held in a viselike grip, she was aware of muscular thighs clamped around her, and a chest like a rock wall at her back. The combination put to rest any notion of wrestling the reins away from the rebel and pushing him to the ground.

"Who are you? Where are you taking me?" she demanded.

"Would you rather go back to Sozar?" The man said in Arabic, his voice muffled by the scarf.

"I'd rather you returned me to the royal lodge. Sheikh Markaz will pay well to get me back."

"Will he?"

The laughter she heard through the scarf raised her

hackles. If Markaz had known where she was, he could well have offered a reward for her return. "Do you doubt me?"

"Only that you're on such intimate terms with the ruler of Nazaar. A short time ago, you were sharing a meal and a fire with the rebel leader."

She shook her tied hands at him. "Does this look as if I was his guest? Anyway, aren't you one of his followers?"

"I'm no one's follower."

"A mercenary, then?" Please don't let him be the interrogator Sozar had summoned, she prayed. The rebel leader had said the man used whatever techniques got results. Was this escapade a ploy to disorientate her before he invaded her mind?

"You ask too many questions."

"Tell me where you're taking me, and I'll stop asking."

"I wish I could count on that."

Not sure she'd heard the muttered comment aright, she lapsed into silence, hearing the harness jangle as the man slowed the horse to a walk. Lather flecked the animal's sides. They would have to stop soon to rest the horse, then she would take off into the desert. This man might not be as uncouth as the other soldiers, but he might still try to take advantage of being alone with her. Perhaps that was his plan all along.

Her stomach roiled, making her thankful she hadn't eaten the food Sozar had offered, so she had nothing to bring up. She breathed slowly until the nausea subsided. "Did Sozar tell you to drag me away, hoping to frighten me into telling him what he wants to know."

"Are you frightened?"

Terrified out of her wits, she thought, but lifted her head defiantly. "Not of you, nor of anything Sozar can do to me." Keeping the fear out of her voice took an effort. She was proud of almost achieving it.

The man pulled the horse up. As he dismounted, she gripped the saddle with her tied hands to keep from falling off. Then his hands spanned her waist and he lifted her to the ground, steadying her when her legs nearly buckled.

The sound of running water nearby suggested they had stopped at a spring. Moonlight glinted off metal as the rebel unsheathed a knife. She tensed, but he only used the blade to strip the rope away from her hands. "No one's following us. You're safe for the moment," he said when he finished.

The rush of restored circulation sent shards of agony flashing into her fingers. She flexed them until the pain eased. "Am I safe from you?"

"You tell me." He unwound the scarf from his face and she dragged in a breath as the eerie light fell on his features.

"Markaz, what are you doing here?"

"Rescuing you, I thought."

In a surge of fury, she balled her abused hand into a fist and swung at his head. He ducked back barely in time, so the blow glanced off his jaw. He rubbed the spot. "What was that for?"

"For letting me think I'd been taken by one of Sozar's men."

"I told you I was no one's man."

"You could have added a name, Your Highness."

His grin flashed whitely. "I needed to be sure you weren't there voluntarily. I couldn't risk being betrayed to the rebels."

Stung by his lack of trust, she touched the ropes dangling from his hand. "Doesn't this tell you anything?"

"I watched Omar let you escape."

"He's not Omar. He's Yusef al Hasa, my half uncle. He let me go after I told him what Sozar had planned for me tomorrow."

Markaz cupped her face. "Is that why you were running away?"

Wildfire tore through her veins. "I had to warn you. Natalie's class ring contains a code to access the weapon your scientists and the Americans have developed. Sozar was bringing in an expert in hypnosis to get the code from my memory. They intend to steal the weapon."

"And use it to bring down my government, I know," Markaz said. "However, the ring won't help him anymore. When the Americans found out Natalie had been killed, they reprogrammed the weapon with new codes. Another agent couriered them to me yesterday."

She must have lost most of one night since being abducted from the royal lodge. "Was that the urgent meeting you left me to attend?"

His voice roughened as he said, "Do you think I'd have left your bed for anything less critical?"

Her throat dried. "I wasn't sure. I…"

"Then be sure of this." He bent his head and took her mouth, kissing her so thoroughly that she was left reeling. Without warning he parted her lips with his tongue and plunged, drinking deeply until her mind blanked to everything but his heat and his strength, and how much she needed both.

His rebel uniform offered the only purchase and she gripped the homespun cloth, holding on as if to reality as the fact of her salvation slammed through her. She could stop acting defiant while falling to pieces inside at the prospect of having her mind plundered. Markaz had come for her. She was safe.

So why didn't she feel safe, instead of as if she stood on the edge of a precipice with nothing underneath to break her fall? Because she wanted him more than she'd ever wanted anything. But the price was too high. So she feasted on his mouth and gloried in his hardness pressing against her, knowing this was all she could allow herself.

Her shudder was strong enough for Markaz to feel, and his arms tightened around her. "It's all right to give in. You were strong when it counted."

Resting briefly against him, she dragged in a ragged breath then lifted her head. "It's not all right. The danger isn't past yet."

His lips whispered over her forehead until her shudders became shivers of longing. "The rebels won't get the weapon. As well as changing the codes, I've doubled the guards around the project."

She hesitated. Finding herself in his arms after thinking she'd never see him again was playing havoc with her thought processes. Hunger for him churned through her, making her want to spread their robes on the powdery sand and take him inside her under the limitless stars. They were hardly the actions of disengagement, but her body wasn't getting the message.

She had actually started to pull him down with her when reason collided with desire. "This isn't only about the weapon. It's personal," she said, hearing her voice thicken with need.

He listened intently, his frown growing as she told him about Sozar being his father's illegitimate son by a foreign nurse working in Nazaar. "The woman feared she'd be deported for posing as the princess, so she didn't tell anyone she was pregnant by your father."

"How does Sozar know his mother didn't make up the story?"

"What matters is that Sozar believes he's your half brother and the true heir to the throne. He's mad with jealousy of you."

From his saddlebag Markaz brought out a water bottle and handed it to her. After she drank, he slaked his own thirst. "If he thinks he's entitled to rule, he's truly mad. A DNA test might prove he has royal blood, but not that my father sired him. If that could be proven, and Sozar was fit to be sheikh, I'd crown him myself."

"Markaz, you can't. He wants to drag Nazaar back into the Dark Ages."

His fingers dug into her arms. "That I will not allow."

"What are you going to do?"

"Hamal and Fayed and their men aren't far behind us. When they get here, we'll strike at the rebel stronghold."

"But the rebels have…"

A hand over her mouth silenced her, and the sheikh pulled her into the shadows. Then she caught the movements his quick hearing had detected. Sozar must have missed her at last, and sent men after them. Until Markaz's men reached them, they were on their own.

Swiftly, silently, Markaz retrieved a rifle from his saddlebag. A knife gleamed in his other hand. She held hers out. With only a slight hesitation, he handed her the knife. The ornate hilt felt cold but reassuring against her palm. Sozar's men would have to kill her to take her back.

She felt Markaz's hand clamp on her shoulder. She leaned her cheek lightly against his hand, then crouched, blade at the ready, running through her mind the drills she'd studied, never expecting to need the skills outside simulated combat. Beside her she saw Markaz steady the rifle along a rock.

Six men approached them. No talk broke their discipline. She hadn't expected that after the night's entertainment. They should have been drunk by now. Perhaps some of the rebels were, but Sozar had sent his best, an ironic compliment.

The cloud cover broke long enough for her to see Sozar himself leading the group. She should have guessed he wouldn't take kindly to losing her, probably adding to his list of grievances against Markaz. His movements were unsteady as a result of the liquor he'd drunk. That could work to their advantage, she thought.

"We need to stall Sozar and give Hamal time to get here," she whispered to Markaz. "Letting him think I'm alone might lower his guard."

"It could also get you shot," Markaz rasped back. "I won't let you sacrifice yourself."

The taut smile she aimed at him was lost in the shadows. "I'm counting on it." She stood up and lifted her hands. "Sozar, I have the information you want. I'll give it to you if you call off your men."

"Tell your rescuer to stand up and show his hands," Sozar instructed.

"He fell from the horse and hit his head. He's unconscious." Markaz started to argue, and she nudged him into silence. "I think he's dead."

The quaver in her voice must have sounded convincing. At Sozar's signal, two of his men emerged from hiding and closed in. Her heart threatened to beat out of her chest. How much longer did Markaz's men need to get here?

Markaz must have had the same thought, because he stood up and his rifle clattered against the rock. "I'm the one you want, Sozar, not the woman. She tells me we're brothers, so we can talk this through."

The other man froze. "Clever. A trap within a trap. But I'm not as stupid as you think." To the rebel closest to him, he said, "Shoot them both."

As the soldier raised his weapon, she felt everything inside her turn arctic. "You won't get the information," she said.

"I don't need the information now that you've delivered Markaz to me. A coward as well as a usurper. He'll be no loss to this country."

Beside her she saw Markaz tense like a snake ready to strike. But his tone was mild as he said, "This doesn't have to end in bloodshed, Sozar. Simone told me how you were wronged at birth. All you have to do is prove your lineage, and the throne is yours."

"I don't have to prove anything to you," Sozar roared. "Once you and that shameless creature with you are dead, I will take what belongs to me."

"You won't do it without a war."

"My men are ready for war."

She saw Markaz's hand move. In one blindingly fast action, his hand closed around the rifle and he fired without lifting the weapon from the rock.

The sound of the shot ricocheted around the canyon, amplified when the rebels answered with their own fire. She was dragged down beside Markaz as he kept shooting. Muzzle flashes lit the darkness, but she couldn't see what was happening until a cloud shifted, revealing Sozar slumped on the ground. An ugly black stain bloomed across the front of his robes.

The battle wasn't over yet. Four of the rebels surged toward their position. Markaz cut one of them down not a yard from Simone. The man fell forward and she grabbed the rifle as it rolled out of his grasp.

For as long as she could remember, her father had

owned guns, insisting she learn how to use them for her own protection. In all the times she'd shot at targets, she'd never expected to find a human being in her sights. Her first shot went wild, then the rifle jammed as a rebel loomed on the rock above them.

"Markaz, look out," she screamed but he was fighting hand-to-hand with another man. Gripping Markaz's knife, she turned as the rebel leaped from the rock above. In the timelessness of the moment she recognized the attacker as Yusef.

Seconds later he was on the ground and she was staring at Yusef's body slumped across the lifeless Sozar. Her knife had been knocked out of her hand. The force of Yusef's leap must have impaled him on the blade, killing him. She turned away as her stomach emptied. Then she felt Markaz's arm around her. When she straightened, he wiped her face clean with her veil, then threw the fabric away. "It's over."

She couldn't look. The image of the man impaled on the knife would be forever etched into her brain. "Yusef is dead. I killed him."

"He's dead, but not by your hand."

The look she shot him was bleak. "He landed on my knife as he jumped from the rocks."

"Yusef may have knocked the knife out of your hand, but Sozar killed him."

"That's not possible. Sozar was already dead."

"He was mortally injured. Before the other man came at me, I saw Sozar groping for his rifle on the ground. Yusef must have seen it, too, and leaped to stop him."

"So he saved your life."

Markaz nodded. "This time for real."

She shuddered as he approached the two bodies, locked

together in a fatal embrace. Moonlight glinted off the clean blade he retrieved from the sand a few feet away from them. When he brought her knife to her, she looked at it in stupefaction. "No matter what he did, I couldn't stand thinking I'd killed him."

His hold didn't slacken. "Killing should never come easily to anyone. I won't forget that you thought you were saving my life."

Then why did she feel so sick and defeated, unable to bring herself to look at the bodies? "Why did you stop me negotiating with Sozar? Didn't you trust me?" Was trust always going to be the issue between them?

"Sozar was the one I didn't trust. While he held your attention, his men were moving up on our flanks."

"So that's why you took over. Not because I'm a woman."

His hands played up and down her arms. She wondered if he was aware of how often he touched her, or that he was doing so now. Or that he started a symphony of needs clamoring for release.

She tamped them down.

The hunger for his possession was no more than the human need to affirm life in the midst of death, she knew. A biological urge to replace lost genes handed down from the cave days. Not appropriate behavior for civilized beings.

Not that she felt civilized now, or ever could around Markaz. Fighting at his side had left her charged with adrenaline. She felt ready to leap out of her own skin. Wanted to lose herself in him until they were both sated. Instead, she held still until his hands dropped away.

Think about returning to Australia, she ordered herself. With Sozar dead, the danger keeping her under Markaz's protection was past. At least she didn't have to tell her mother that she'd caused Yusef's death.

Markaz guessed her thoughts. "You can tell your mother that her relative died a hero. I can't damn him for defending his beliefs."

She finally made herself look at her half uncle's body. "How can a country grow strong by denying half its population the chance to reach their full potential?"

"Short answer? It can't." He took her arm again and steered her away from the carnage. She stiffened, but told herself the touch was clinical, for her good. So why did desire leap inside her like a startled gazelle? This was getting crazy. She couldn't even fight at his side without wanting him. He might agree that women deserved equal opportunity, but he was still the sheikh, the take-charge leader. And she had never wanted him more.

The growl of car engines made her heartbeat stutter. As if to prove her point, Markaz grabbed the rifle and stepped between her and the new arrivals. But this time it was the cavalry. Hamal and Fayed and their men poured from the vehicles and stared at the downed rebels. "We were closing in when we heard the battle," Fayed explained. "But it looks as if we aren't needed."

Lowering the weapon, Markaz shook his head. "There's still the rebel enclave. Simone saw a dozen men in training not far from here. They'll have heard the gunfire, too, and be expecting trouble. We'll have our work cut out for us."

"It will be a pleasure, Your Highness," Hamal promised. "I'll detail a man to escort Sima to safety."

Simone stepped around Markaz. "I'm not going anywhere. I want to see this through to the end."

Seeing that Simone wouldn't be swayed, Markaz reached a decision. "We'll all go. Makes the numbers a bit more even."

"I thought you'd have had enough bloodshed for one day," he said to Simone as they neared the rebel camp. There was no need for stealth since the gun battle would already have alerted the remaining rebels.

"Isn't my behavior feminine enough for you?" she asked.

He restrained a sigh. If she was risking her beautiful neck to prove something to him about women's lib, there was no need. "As soon as we're back at the lodge, we're going to talk," he stated. This had gone far enough.

Fighting beside him, she'd demonstrated her equality once and for all. She had nothing to prove to him. But maybe she had something to prove to herself. He massaged his chin thoughtfully. Focusing on his feelings for her, was he missing the point? She had been taken and held hostage by the rebels. Had she chosen to go back to the camp because she needed to face her captors?

His admiration for her grew. No, damn it. His love for her. He could no longer deny the truth to himself. He loved her. Knowing she despised his country's ways, the thought was pure agony. Letting her go when this was over would be harder than anything he'd ever done.

The battle was short and surprisingly unbloody. As Markaz had suspected, the rebels were waiting, guns ready, when his squad approached. But drink and revelry had slowed their response times. Hamal's men soon had them subdued and disarmed, rounded up in one of their own training corrals.

Hearing that Sozar was dead also sapped their spirits. Markaz had the feeling most of them would soon renounce their support of the rebel cause.

"I'll check the tents to make sure there are no hidden snipers," he said. He knew better than to tell Simone to stay behind him, but felt happier when she fell into step beside him of her own accord.

"Feeling better?" he asked her as he jabbed the flap of the first tent open with his rifle barrel.

"Why should I? You think I enjoyed the fight?"

The tent was empty. "I think you needed this."

Her bewildered expression almost had him taking her in his arms. He resisted, moving on to the next tent. "By turning the tables on your abductors, you've proved to yourself that you're not helpless."

She looked thoughtful. "Perhaps you're right. Most of my life I was coddled by my father. Having lost his home, he was desperate not to lose anything or anyone else precious to him. I went along because I understood, but I always wondered how I'd handle myself in a crisis."

He jabbed the next tent flap open. Nothing. "And now you know."

"Yes. Markaz, watch out."

He'd already caught the stir of movement in the tent, and had the rifle cocked and ready. "Come out with your hands showing," he ordered.

The rebel had been trying to escape through the back of the tent. Now he raised his hands and came out.

Simone gasped. "It's a woman. While I was a prisoner, I didn't see any other women in the camp."

Markaz gestured with the rifle. "Are you Sozar's woman? Let us see your face."

Slowly the rebel unwound the scarf from her features, and Markaz froze in shock. "What the hell are you doing here?"

"Waiting for my son," Princess Norah said calmly.

The sheikh stared at his mother in disbelief. "What do you mean, you're waiting for me? Are you a hostage, too? Was this supposed to be a trap?"

Then clarity struck Simone like lightning. "She doesn't mean you, Markaz. She means her son, Sozar. You were the foreign nurse who posed as the princess to seduce Sheikh Kemal all those years ago, weren't you?"

Norah's defiant expression softened. "I was in love with him from the first time I saw him. But I was afraid if Kemal found out I'd deceived him, he'd have been angry enough to send me back to America. So I kept my condition secret, not hard to do under these robes. I'd gone to the clinic under a false name, and left without knowing my child still lived. Thinking he was dead, I couldn't tell Kemal what I'd done because I didn't want him to hate me as much as I hated myself."

Markaz looked thunderstruck. "Sozar was your son?"

"I didn't know he was alive until I stumbled on him and Omar meeting in secret when I was out walking. At first, when Sozar told me who he was, I didn't believe him. But his adoptive mother had told him details known only to someone who'd been at the clinic that day. While medicated, I'd apparently blurted out the truth about his conception, except for my identity. At least I had the sense to keep that to myself." She pulled in a deep breath. "His adopted parents had told him some of his history. They assumed it was a fantasy, but Sozar believed it from the first. He did some checking, and deduced that I had to be his mother."

Sozar had needed to believe he was of royal blood, Simone thought. "So he really was the true heir to the throne?"

Norah paled. "He's dead, isn't he?"

Markaz didn't flinch from the truth. "I killed him after he attacked Simone and me."

"A kind of justice, I suppose. He promised me you

wouldn't be hurt, only tried and exiled. I wouldn't have helped him otherwise. I love you too much."

"Sozar had other plans. Mother, how could you be so ill-advised?"

Her pale features suggested she was in shock. Markaz looked as if he wasn't far behind her. "Love makes one do stupid things. Sometimes you spend your whole life paying for them," she said.

"But how could you side with the rebels after they killed my father and brother?"

Norah braced herself against the tent pole. "Sozar swore that he had nothing to do with the violent faction responsible for killing Kemal and Esan. Sozar insisted he wanted peaceful change. I supported him because it's what I want, too." She reached to touch her youngest son's face, but he shied away. "Like your father, you can't see that Nazaar is perfect as it is."

"Nazaar is so perfect you couldn't keep your baby without being deported," he said bitterly. "That wouldn't have happened in a truly free country."

The princess covered her face with her hands and her shoulders shook. Simone touched Markaz. "I think she knows."

He looked at the silently sobbing woman. "Alert the others. We're getting out of here."

Chapter 16

A lot had happened in the month since they'd returned to the palace at Raisa, Simone reflected. As soon as the squad and their rebel prisoners had reached the royal lodge, Markaz had ordered the household back to the city. The motorcade had been a grim one. At his command, Simone had traveled with Markaz, but he had spoken little on the journey, and she'd had no idea how to reach him.

Norah had traveled in her own car as a captive this time, then had been confined to her apartment at her palace. After her confession at the rebel camp, she'd refused to say any more outside a courtroom.

Expressing her disbelief that Norah was involved with the rebels, Amal had hardly been able to stop talking about the news. "Few of us really liked Norah, but she's the last person we suspected of being a traitor," she'd observed.

Simone had agreed. "Sozar must have been using her to get even for what she'd done to him."

"Do you think Natalie had also uncovered Norah's link with Sozar?" Amal had asked.

"It's possible, although Norah denies being involved in the murder. According to her, Sozar's group wanted peaceful change. She seems to be in denial about everything to do with him."

Amal had nodded. "At least you know why Sozar was after you. He must have known you'd seen him speak to Norah in the parking lot at Al-Qasr."

"I didn't know who she was then. When she entertained me at lunch, I felt as if I'd seen her somewhere before, but couldn't place where. I wish I'd made the connection sooner." If she had, less blood might have been spilled.

Now Simone and Amal were drinking mint tea together for possibly the last time while Norah's trial was underway in the hall of justice not far away.

As a key witness, Simone had remained in the country, and had accepted the sheikh's invitation to continue living at the palace. She hadn't been able to look at Markaz when she identified Norah as the woman she'd seen talking to Sozar at Al-Qasr.

Unbalanced by the deaths of her husband and son, Norah had seen Sozar's return as a miracle, her oldest son restored to her after years of believing she'd killed him in that medical clinic.

"How horrible to live with such guilt for so long," Simone commented. "She must be unbalanced to believe that Sozar's plans were peaceful. She said she didn't want anyone to get hurt."

Amal snorted. "What did she think the rebels were

doing in that training camp? As a hostage, you must have been terrified, wondering what would happen to you."

"I never stopped believing I would escape, or that Markaz's men would find me."

"You didn't expect him to turn up in person? You must mean a lot to him."

Bitterness gripped Simone. "Enough that he's putting me on his private plane back to Australia now that the trial is almost concluded." The verdict was due to be handed down later today, so she would be leaving to-morrow. She should finish packing, but couldn't summon the will.

Markaz had disqualified himself from presiding over his mother's trial, but had sat through every moment of the evidence. The news that he was sending Simone home had been delivered during a recess. Except for that brief ex-change, she hadn't seen him alone since they'd been back at the palace.

Simone couldn't decide which hurt worse: his decision or the matter-of-fact way he'd told her. For all the emotion he showed, the scene in the secret room at the desert lodge might never have taken place. Yet she couldn't erase the memory from her mind. No matter what happened to her in future, she would never forget the paradise she'd found in his arms. Or stop longing for more.

Amal looked shocked. "Markaz can't mean to let you go after all that's happened."

"He thinks it's for my own good. After his experience with Natalie and now with Norah, he's convinced I'm better off returning to Australia."

"What do you think?"

"He could be right."

"How can you say that? You love him, don't you?"

Miserably, Simone nodded. "With all my heart." If his lovemaking hadn't been enough, fighting at his side in the desert had convinced her beyond any doubt.

"Have you told him how you feel?"

"With the trial, there hasn't been the chance."

"You mean you haven't made the chance. You've managed to keep your business going, haven't you?"

Simone couldn't deny that. Too heartsick to do anything else, she'd turned to work for comfort. According to Drew, introducing the range of Nazaari designs had tripled the orders and led to an unexpected invitation from a cable TV show to do a story about Simone's travels.

If she told them everything, it would be quite a scoop, she thought. She hadn't even shared the whole story with her mother, although they'd spoken on the phone every day since Simone returned to Raisa.

Hearing that Yusef had died saving the sheikh's life had been a turning point for Sara. According to her caregiver, Sara's depression had started to lift soon after she learned of his fate from Simone.

At least some good had come of the adventure, Simone consoled herself. "I needed to occupy my time," she told Amal. "As for Markaz, fate has other plans for me."

"Never mind fate. What about your plans for you?"

"I'm going to come back to the Middle East and expand our range of designs from the region."

Amal made a sound of frustration. "Not your business plans, your life. You can't give up on Markaz now."

"He's the one giving up on me."

"Then you must change his mind. Do you think my fiancé knew straight away that we were meant to be together? I had to work hard to convince him."

In spite of her aching heart, Simone laughed. "I'm

starting to wonder if Nazaari women need the law changing to let you share in running this country. You seem to be doing well enough in your own way already."

Her friend preened as if at a compliment. "When you don't have a legal voice in public affairs, you find ways to influence matters behind the scenes."

"All the same, wouldn't you rather express your opinions openly?"

"We shall, as soon as Markaz's final reforms are put to a vote."

The sheikh had decreed that would happen as soon as his committee of advisors had framed the legislation they'd been working on during the preceding year. Having had enough of bloodshed from a minority opposed to change, he'd announced he was holding the first referendum in Nazaari history to give his people a say in the kind of future they wanted. He had promised to abide by the results of the vote.

The people would support him, Simone believed. Since the destruction of the rebel stronghold, there had been no more signs of revolt against the throne. The people seemed happy to have any opposition aired in council, rather than at gunpoint.

Not even fighting alongside him had convinced Markaz she belonged with him. If anything, it had made him more determined to send her back where he believed she belonged. The only conclusion she could reach was that he didn't return her love.

She got to her feet. "The verdict is due this afternoon. I'd better go and pack."

Amal stood up. "Then I'll help you, against my better judgment."

Against her own, too, Simone thought. It came to her

that she was reliving in part her parents' departure from Nazaar, without the threat of danger. Was longing for a place they couldn't have part of her inheritance?

Not a place, a man. Her feelings weren't for Markaz as monarch of a country, or even to the country itself. If he were an ordinary man in an ordinary place, she would still love him more than she knew how to express.

"You don't have to subject yourself to every minute of the trial," Fayed told the sheikh. The judges, members of Markaz's advisory council, were in recess to consider their verdict. Fayed had followed Markaz into the antechamber he used when presiding over the majlis. From his friend's worried expression, Markaz guessed he must look as haggard as he felt.

"What else can I do? The defendant is my mother," he said.

Fayed frowned. "I should have guessed Princess Norah was up to something. All those long walks she took outside the palace, insisting she needed to be alone, were really to meet with Sozar."

"Hard to believe we were brothers." Or how different his life could have turned out if Norah had kept her first-born son. Sozar would have become the sheikh.

And Markaz would be free to follow his heart.

He drove the thought away. The sheikh was never free of duty, and his was to marry a woman of his own kind who would give the country an heir. He'd married for love once, and look what happened.

His reality didn't…couldn't include Simone. However much he loved her, he had to send her away for her sake and the good of his country.

The pain in his heart was almost more than he could stand.

* * *

Simone straightened, the galabia Amal had pressed upon her as a gift, drifting out of her hands. "I can't do this. I can't leave Nazaar. Markaz may not want me, but he can't make me go. I've done nothing to deserve being thrown out of the country." Except fall in love with the sheikh, she thought. Foolish in the extreme, but hardly a crime.

Amal smiled. "Now you're talking. When will you tell Markaz?"

"Right now." Before her courage deserted her, Simone decided. The verdict in Norah's trial was about to be announced. Markaz would need someone with him when he received the news. She could be his friend, if not his lover, Simone told herself. If her heart threatened to beat out of her chest at the prospect of being with him, unable to touch him or feel his mouth on hers ever again, that was her problem.

When she reached the hall of justice, the majlis was in recess. Markaz was in his private antechamber adjoining the hall, Fayed told her. As usual, the bodyguard was keeping an eye on everything, the sheikh's rock of reliability. Since she'd helped to destroy the rebel camp, Fayed had treated her like a daughter. In turn, her affection for the big man had also grown.

"Can I see him?"

Fayed's dark brows came together. "He has not asked to see you." His rumbling tone was gentle.

"If I wait until then, the Lost Quarter will have frozen over. He needs me, Fayed. At least until the trial is over."

"You would go to him as a friend, no matter the cost to yourself?"

He understood, she thought, the pressure around her heart almost intolerable. "I can't be anything more."

Fayed nodded. "A friend will do."

He escorted her down the long hall, past a table brimming with gifts sent by the people to their sheikh as an outpouring of their support. Baskets of their most perfect fruit, ceramic flagons of juice from their own presses and handwoven cloth were all carefully labeled with the sender's name.

The sheikh swiveled from a console littered with papers, his mouth tightening when he saw her. While she hadn't expected a welcome, he had no cause to be angry with her.

This room was a far cry from the austere room off the hall of justice at Karama. Thick Persian carpets padded the marble floor, the furnishings were Arabian antiques and there was no blank wall leading to a secret love nest.

The sheikh saw her eyes go to where the door was in the other chamber. If his thoughts also flashed back to what they had shared in the secret room, he gave no outward sign. Nor did he seem to notice that she was unveiled. He had recently decreed that none of the women were required to wear veils now. None too soon for Simone. "Is there a problem with your flight?" he asked.

"No problem. I asked your pilot to delay the flight until after the verdict is announced."

"Then let me save you any more delay. My mother will be found guilty of consorting with the rebels and sentenced to exile in America. She still has American citizenship and family there, so she will not be without resources. But she will not be permitted to return to Nazaar."

Simone had meant to be supportive, but couldn't help resentment spilling over. "You can't wait for me to leave, too, can you? Do you blame me for your mother's downfall?"

He looked surprised. "I blame no one but my mother herself. She set these events in motion when she deceived my father even after she married him. The rebellion may have happened anyway, but there's no doubt her actions gave the rebels their leader."

He seemed to be waiting for her to go, but her feet felt glued to the floor. "Is the rebellion over now?" she asked, more for an excuse to remain than because she wanted to continue the discussion. She shouldn't have come. Packing and leaving without seeing him again would have been the sensible thing to do. Being so close to him when he couldn't wait to be rid of her was sheer torture.

All she could think of was how much she ached to be in his arms. They were closed to her now, his demeanor remote. "The rebellion ended some time ago. Sozar kept the desert camp going with only a small group of recruits, believing more followers would join them in time. He couldn't accept that he and his group were the last of a dying breed." Markaz tapped a paper on the console. "A few diehards will have to be rooted out, like the madman behind this threat."

She took a few steps closer, ignoring the warning signs flashing in his eyes. "What threat?"

He showed her a page made up of words cut from newspaper. "According to this, if my mother is found guilty, he'll blow up the palace."

Her senses sharpened. "You're taking the threat seriously, of course?"

"The original letter is with the police for forensic examination. They believe they are close to tracking down the sender. Before today's court convened, Hamal's people searched the palace and grounds. They found nothing untoward."

"They didn't suspect Norah, either." Her voice felt strained. "Don't go into the hall of justice to hear the verdict. Let Fayed bring word to you here."

He pushed to his feet. "No matter what my mother has done, I will not deny her my presence."

She tried to step in his way, but his hands clamped around her arms and she was moved aside effortlessly. "Markaz, please. I have a bad feeling about this."

"The bad feeling you have is between us. Don't mix it up with anything else."

"I don't have a bad feeling about us," she snapped. "How can I, when making love with you was the most amazing experience of my life?"

She waited for him to argue, but his long lashes shuttered his eyes. When he looked up, there was only regal hardness. "Consider it a unique souvenir of your time in Nazaar."

Determined not to flinch, she kept her head up. "No I won't, because I'm not leaving."

"Your departure is by my command. Have you forgotten who I am?"

"Not for an instant. But even the sheikh can't expel a citizen who's done nothing wrong."

He dragged a hand down his face. "I can't deny your right to citizenship through your parents. But what do you gain by staying?"

"The chance to prove that you're sending me away for the wrong reason."

She had his full attention now. "Go on."

"You were so badly burned by Natalie hating this country, and now by your mother turning traitor that you're determined not to make the same mistake again. So I'm going to show you that I belong here." With you, she thought but didn't say.

His eyes narrowed. "What about your mother?"

"Since I told her that Yusef died a hero, she's improved steadily. According to her caregiver, there's a certain friend who has been visiting her every day. Reading to her, taking her for walks and spending time with her. Her progress has as much to do with him, as with knowing what happened to Yusef. If this goes where I think it will, she won't need me holding her hand."

"Go home, Simone," Markaz said tiredly.

"I am home." The sooner he realized that, the better for both of them.

A discreet knock was followed by Fayed's appearance. "The judges are returning to the hall, Your Highness. They are ready to pronounce their verdict."

"Thank you." When the door closed, Markaz turned to her. "I can't stop you living here, but it doesn't change anything. When this is over I shall take a Nazaari-born wife and provide the country with an heir as is my duty. You would do well to return to Australia and do yours."

"Don't lecture me on duty," she whispered but was talking to herself. The door to the antechamber swished shut as Markaz returned to the hall.

Frustration burned through her. Snatching up a priceless ceramic flagon, she nearly pitched it at the closed door, stopping herself barely in time. The men in her life were good at knowing what was best for her. Until now she'd gone along, but not anymore. "I'm staying, get used to it," she yelled, the sound swallowed by the thick walls and Persian carpets.

Slowly she lowered the flagon then stared at it, her blood turning to ice. She knew. Oh God, she knew where the bomb was hidden.

The flagon fell from her nerveless fingers as she launched herself at the door. The hall was filled with people. Most were men in traditional robes, but she saw a few of the royal woman, unveiled and looking subdued

at witnessing the historic trial. Amal was among them
and tried to get Simone's attention, but she had eyes only
for Markaz.

He was conferring with the presiding judge, a high
official from his council, she recalled. The two of them
stood near the table of gifts. Norah was led past them
under guard. Without looking at his mother, Markaz
moved to his seat, and silence was called for.

Simone tried to reach him through the throng, but a
cordon of security barred her way. Terror lodged in her
throat. If she screamed her suspicion, she would be
dragged out before she could make herself understood.
She had to stay calm. Ignore the pounding of fear in her
head. "Hamal," she called in an undertone.

The security chief turned. "Be silent. The judge is
about to speak."

Controlling her voice, she said, "This can't wait. The
sheikh's life is in danger. The letter isn't a hoax. While I
was a hostage, I saw the rebels making olive oil flagons
into bombs."

His gaze flashed from her to the table of gifts and she
saw comprehension dawn. "Clear the majlis now," he
ordered, his voice ringing with authority. A moment of
stunned silence ensued, followed by shrieks of panic from
the women as the security men started to rush everyone
out. She saw Markaz directing the magistrates to safety.

Fayed tried to steer her out also, but she shook off his
arm. "I'm not going anywhere until Markaz leaves." The
giant wasted no time arguing, instead joining Hamal and
the men searching the table. The pungent scent of cold-
pressed oil filled the hall as harmless flagons shattered.

"You should go," Markaz said, moving to her side.

"So should you. Your people need you alive."

"If there is a bomb." His tone was dubious. "All the gifts were screened by security."

"It's there." She would stake her life on it. Was doing so, in fact.

"I've found it. The security tag on this one is a fake."

Horror clawed through her as Fayed gingerly isolated a flagon, a gift of death from the last of the rebels. Indistinguishable from the others except for an odd glass bulge protruding below the security tape.

Markaz tensed. "Can you disarm it?"

Fayed shook his head. "There is nothing to disarm. The seal contains a bulb of acid designed to seep through, completing a circuit and triggering an explosion. We have to get out now."

Her feet were moving even as she heard Markaz bark the order. His arm around her almost lifted her off her feet, propelling her toward the exit as Hamal and Fayed surged with them. Too far, she thought. Now she wouldn't be sent away after all.

Heat slammed into her back and her lungs emptied of air. A roaring sound filled her ears. Her world turned upside down, blackness eclipsing the sight of Markaz throwing himself between her and a wall of flame.

"Sima, open your eyes."

Fingers prized up her eyelids, and pinpoints of light invaded the peaceful place where she'd retreated from the reality of Markaz's death. He'd sacrificed himself to save her, unaware that her heart had died with him.

"Please, my beauty, wake up."

Shock jolted through her. Then a joy so intense it was close to pain. She opened her eyes, feasting on the sight of Markaz leaning over her. Behind him was Dr. Rakha, but her blurred vision could only accommodate the sheikh. "You're alive." She reached out, touching him the only therapy she needed. "The explosion…you came between me and the fire."

"Only singed. I'll recover."

Then she saw the blackened sleeve of his robe falling away from his reddened arm. "Does it hurt?"

"Not as much as the thought of losing you."

The doctor coughed. "I've done all I can for you two, for the moment. With your permission, Your Highness, I'll tend to my other patients."

"Are you sure Simone will be all right?"

"I'll monitor her for signs of concussion, but she should be fine."

After Markaz dismissed the doctor, she struggled to sit up. She was lying on a couch in Markaz's office. "Who else was hurt?"

"Hamal was knocked out by the blast, and Fayed sustained minor burns. Nothing worse, thanks to your warning about the flagon. One of my mother's guards who'd remained loyal to her, was seen placing a flagon onto the table of gifts. The police already suspected that the threatening letter originated inside the palace, and were closing in on him. He died in the explosion."

"And your mother?"

"She was taken to safety."

"Then the danger is finally over."

He nodded. "The majlis will reconvene shortly to give their verdict, putting an end to the rebellion once and for all."

And to Markaz's relationship with his mother if she was deported as expected. Simone ached for him. "This must be hard for you."

"Yes, but harder when I thought you'd been killed." He perched on the edge of the bed and pulled her into his arms. "I thought I could send you away and still go on. Now I know I can't."

Her stomach unknotted a little. "I told you I wasn't going anywhere. I love Nazaar."

"What about her sheikh?"

"He's more of a challenge. He can be the most arrogant, domineering…"

The rest was drowned by his mouth closing over hers. The room swam. When he allowed her up for air, she was panting. "See what I mean? I can't express an opinion without being silenced."

"Express another one," he insisted, his smile provocative.

Her heart leaped. "I'm done."

"I'm not." He kissed her again slowly and deeply, parting her lips and exploring like a deep-sea diver entering a newly discovered cavern filled with wonders. Lights danced at the fringes of her vision. If this was concussion, she could handle any amounts of it, she decided.

Her brow creased in sudden concern. "I'm not unconscious and dreaming, am I?"

He nipped her lower lip. "You were only out for a little while." Then he looked into her eyes. "Vision normal, pupils a little enlarged in response to stimulation."

Her arms linked around his neck. "What do you prescribe for my condition?"

He didn't hesitate. "Marriage."

Her heartbeat double-timed. "A few hours ago, you were putting me on a plane to Australia. Now you're proposing marriage?"

"A few hours ago, I was a fool."

She touched her fingers to his lips, inhaling sharply as his teeth closed around the tips. "Don't talk that way about the man I love."

His expression became serious. "Even though he tried to send you away?"

"You thought you were doing the right thing. You may still regret taking on an independent-minded Australian."

"She is also half-Nazaari desert warrior," he reminded her. "Two women for the price of one."

"In that case, you won't need a harem after we're married. I don't intend to share you," she warned.

His mouth curved. "I need only you, if you'll have me."

She threaded her fingers through his hair, tugging his head down to plunder his mouth. "From the moment I saw you at Al-Qasr, there was never the slightest doubt. I love you, my sheikh of sheikhs."

"And I will cherish your love, as I cherish you," he promised. "As my princess, you'll rule at my side. And when my final reforms are passed, you'll lead the women of Nazaar into their future."

Her breath gusted out. "This princess business is scary territory for me."

He kissed the tip of her nose. "Don't worry. I will teach you everything you need to know."

Thinking of how much he had already taught her, she slanted him a wicked look. "Everything? You mean there's more?"

Like hers, his thoughts had spun back to the secret chamber where their love had first blossomed, she saw from the glint in his eye. He lifted her hand and kissed her knuckles, his gaze holding hers as he said, "My beauty, we have barely begun."

Epilogue

"Are those people out of their minds?" Simone's grip on Markaz's hand was so tight that her nails dug crescent marks into his palm.

He endured stoically. "We expected the vote in Karama to be divided on the reforms. The province was the last holdout of the rebel movement," he reminded her, bemused by her interest in the referendum.

Her brow beaded and she closed her eyes, then opened them wider. "Can't you impose martial law or something, make them see reason?"

He laughed. "Hardly, my love. The point of the voting is to let the people choose their own future."

Her words came out separated by little puffs of breath. "Even—if—they—don't—know—what's—good—for—them?"

The broadcast switched back to the studio, and the

woman presenter launched a rundown of the voting so far. Not long ago, she would have been veiled even on camera. Now her exotic beauty shone down the lens without impediment. Not as lovely as his Simone, he thought, unable to take his eyes off his wife. After ten months of marriage, she was still the most gorgeous woman he knew. Beautiful as she'd been with her hair dark, he adored that she'd returned to her natural golden coloring.

In the background, the presenter announced that only in Karama were Markas's reforms meeting any opposition. The vote was still in his favor, although by a smaller margin than elsewhere. There was no longer any doubt. The new laws had received overwhelming support throughout Nazaar.

When this was confirmed, a cheer went up around the room and Simone smiled through clenched teeth. "You did it."

"We did it," he amended. The women of Nazaar were now legally the equal of their menfolk in everything.

At his gesture, the television was turned off. "The people were inspired by their princess's example. They would do anything for you," he told his wife.

Her back arched. "They're welcome to do this," she said between panting breaths. "Next time it's your turn."

He covered her hand with both of his. "You know if it were possible, I would trade places with you in a heartbeat."

With a mighty, strangled cry that almost shattered his heart, she reared off the bed, her lovely features crumpling with strain. At the foot of the bed, Dr. Rakha bent to his work, then straightened. In his hands he held a mottled, squirming bundle that he placed on Simone's heaving chest. "Congratulations, Your Highnesses. You have a perfect daughter."

Markaz swabbed Simone's brow, sharing her entrancement at the tiny creature nuzzling Simone. In wonder, she touched the head strewn with damp black hair. "Look, she has your coloring. Isn't she the most beautiful girl in the world?"

His eyes swam and his heart swelled. He looked from the baby to Simone. "She is beautiful, but the title has already been claimed," he said, his voice thickening as he stroked the side of Simone's face. He reached out and the baby curled her tiny hand around his finger. Only reflex at this stage, he knew, but he felt as if his daughter was greeting him.

He was a father. He could hardly believe it. After spending the last few months convincing himself that Simone was his to love and cherish for the rest of their lives, now his love expanded to include their baby. Just as well love was infinite.

Suddenly Simone reached for him again, her face contorting with pain. "Markaz," she cried on a rising note of renewed suffering, her free hand cradling the baby while Simone clung to Markaz with a deathly grip.

Dr. Rakha looked unworried as he leaned over her again. "About time her little brother decided to join us."

A nurse took their daughter while Simone labored. Then the doctor was holding their second child and Markaz thought his heart would burst. They had twins, a daughter and a son, both perfect.

He kissed Simone's forehead. "Well done, my love."

Her dreamy smile rewarded him. "You, too." The doctor filled Simone's arms with the babies. She beamed at them. "This is your daddy, little ones. He's just won a huge vote of support from his people. They love him."

Markaz could hardly breathe. "Not as much as I love you and our children."

He saw her eyes struggle to stay open. "I love you so much," she murmured. Then she drifted and he watched over his family, oblivious to the medical activity continuing quietly around them.

"What?" he demanded, catching Dr. Rakha's wry look. "Something in my eyes made them water, that's all."

The doctor was handing him a box of tissues. "Of course, Your Highness. Happens a lot in here." Their work done, he ushered his team out of the room.

Simone stirred, gazing at Markaz so tenderly that he stopped caring if his emotions brimmed over. Even a sheikh was entitled to get emotional at a time like this, he told himself. He wrapped his arms around his wife and babies, holding them where they would always belong, close to his heart.

* * * * *

FIRST CAME THE COVER-UP... THEN CAME THE NIGHTMARE

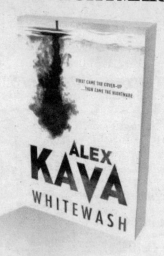

Florida
Investigating the disappearance of her boss, scientist Sabrina Gallows discovers a deadly secret that her employers will kill to keep hidden.

Washington, DC
Congressional aide Jason Brill suspects his boss's friendship with big business may be more of a liability than an asset.

Together, Sabrina and Jason are drawn into a sinister plot that puts corporate greed and corruption above human life. Each must race against time to reveal the truth about this unspeakable evil...

Available 21st March 2008

www.mirabooks.co.uk

MIRA

Celebrate 100 years of pure reading pleasure with Mills & Boon®

To mark our centenary, each month we're publishing a special 100th Birthday Edition. These celebratory editions are packed with extra features and include a FREE bonus story.

Now that's worth celebrating!

4th January 2008

The Vanishing Viscountess by Diane Gaston
With FREE story The Mysterious Miss M
This award-winning tale of the Regency Underworld launched Diane Gaston's writing career.

1st February 2008

Cattle Rancher, Secret Son by Margaret Way
With FREE story His Heiress Wife
Margaret Way excels at rugged Outback heroes…

15th February 2008

Raintree: Inferno by Linda Howard
With FREE story Loving Evangeline
A double dose of Linda Howard's heady mix of passion and adventure.

Don't miss out! From February you'll have the chance to enter our fabulous monthly prize draw. See special 100th Birthday Editions for details.

www.millsandboon.co.uk

FREE!
4 Books
and a surprise gift!

We would like to take this opportunity to thank you for reading this Mills & Boon® book by offering you the chance to take FOUR more specially selected titles from the Intrigue series absolutely FREE! We're also making this offer to introduce you to the benefits of the Mills & Boon® Reader Service™—

- ★ FREE home delivery
- ★ FREE gifts and competitions
- ★ FREE monthly Newsletter
- ★ Exclusive Reader Service offers
- ★ Books available before they're in the shops

Accepting these FREE books and gift places you under no obligation to buy, you may cancel at any time, even after receiving your free shipment. Simply complete your details below and return the entire page to the address below. You don't even need a stamp!

YES! Please send me 4 free Intrigue books and a surprise gift. I understand that unless you hear from me, I will receive 6 superb new titles every month for just £3.15 each, postage and packing free. I am under no obligation to purchase any books and may cancel my subscription at any time. The free books and gift will be mine to keep in any case.

18ZEF

Ms/Mrs/Miss/Mr ....Initials...........................

BLOCK CAPITALS PLEASE

Surname ....

Address...

....

....Postcode ....

Send this whole page to:
UK: FREEPOST CN8I, Croydon, CR9 3WZ